"Something wrong?"

Daniel's soft question startled Angelica. She swallowed back her automatic denial, saying, "Not really. I was just wishing I hadn't stopped for that meal."

"Because it made you ill, or because the illness made you dependent on me?"

"No one likes to feel dependent on a stranger," she responded guardedly. But as he leaned across to take her empty cup, she flinched back automatically.

"Is it because I'm a stranger, or because I'm a man?" Daniel asked her bluntly. "Is that the reason you're so anxious to move next door, even though both of us know damn well that you're not strong enough?"

"No," she denied, horrified by what he was saying. The truth was...it was herself she was afraid of. Her own reactions, her own needs—needs that she felt were getting out of hand....

PENNY JORDAN was constantly in trouble in school because of her inability to stop daydreaming—especially during French lessons. In her teens, she was an avid romance reader, although it didn't occur to her to try writing one herself until she was older. "My first half-dozen attempts ended up ingloriously," she remembers, "but I persevered, and one manuscript was finished." She plucked up the courage to send it to a publisher, convinced her book would be rejected. It wasn't, and the rest is history! Penny is married and lives in Cheshire.

Penny Jordan's striking mainstream novel *Power Play* quickly became a *New York Times* bestseller. She followed that success with *Silver,* a story of ambition, passion and intrigue and *The Hidden Years,* a novel that lays bare the choices all women face in their search for love.

Books by Penny Jordan

HARLEQUIN PRESENTS
1369—BITTER BETRAYAL
1388—BREAKING AWAY
1404—UNSPOKEN DESIRE
1418—RIVAL ATTRACTIONS
1427—OUT OF THE NIGHT
1442—GAME OF LOVE

HARLEQUIN SIGNATURE EDITION
LOVE'S CHOICES
STRONGER THAN YEARNING

PENNY JORDAN

second time loving

Harlequin Books

TORONTO • NEW YORK • LONDON
AMSTERDAM • PARIS • SYDNEY • HAMBURG
STOCKHOLM • ATHENS • TOKYO • MILAN
MADRID • WARSAW • BUDAPEST • AUCKLAND

Harlequin Presents first edition July 1992
ISBN 0-373-11476-1

Original hardcover edition published in 1990
by Mills & Boon Limited

SECOND TIME LOVING

CHAPTER ONE

NOT far now. Angelica had just driven through the last village on Tom's list, and, according to the route he had worked out for her, the lane to the cottage should only be a couple of miles ahead of her.

She was glad that the drive from London was nearly over. Her back was stiff with tension, her eyes gritty and tired. Tired... She smiled cynically to herself. Eighteen months ago, even twelve months ago, if anyone had told her that tiredness, exhaustion, both physical and mental, and most of all emotional was going to overrun and dominate her entire life she would have laughed at them. But then she hadn't known what she knew now: that this numbing, destructive, all-encompassing form of exhaustion, this longing to close her eyes, curl up in a small ball to sleep and go on sleeping was a form of depression as dangerous and invasive in its way as its far more publicised and recognised cousins.

She had learned an awful lot during these last eighteen months though, too much perhaps, and certainly a good deal that she would rather not have learned. Her mouth twisted painfully. She ought to have remembered that old adage about there being no fool like an old one; not that at twenty-eight she was old precisely, even though if, right at this moment, she felt as though she were inhabiting the body of a

woman thirty years her senior rather than one sup-
posedly at the height of her mental and sexual peak.

Her sexual peak. The twist of her mouth became
even more pronounced. In these days of increasing
concern over and responsiveness to the growing threat
of AIDS, it was perhaps not the stigma it had once
been to be a woman of over twenty-one with so limited
a sexual history that she was still actually a virgin,
but it was still something she preferred to keep to
herself; a vulnerable Achilles' heel, in someone who,
to the rest of her small world at least, was the subject
of admiration and envy.

When she had first taken over her father's ailing
business, manufacturing an old-fashioned brand of
face cream and cleansers supplied on a mail-order
basis to a very limited list of customers, she had done
so because she had no alternative. When she was fresh
from serving her articles with a firm of accountants,
and had just passed her exams, her father's sudden
heart attack and death had left her mother solely dependent on an income from a company which had
become more and more precariously financially based.

It had been a chance conversation with a friend
which had led to her turning round the whole focus
of the company, so that instead of marketing its tra-
ditional products Angelica had taken the huge risk of
completely reorganising the company and marketing
products which were based entirely on natural
ingredients.

There had been no time for careful market re-
search; no time to do anything other than make her
decision and then act upon it.

The success of the company was something that sometimes surprised even her. It had expanded to such an extent that she had had to invest in new factory premises and an increased work-force, and had taken on the kind of financial and emotional burdens that went with economic success.

And yet she had thrived on it, revelled in the challenge. When others flagged, she had laughed at them; when others doubted, she had stuck to the force of her own convictions and been proved right.

Her mother was now living very comfortably indeed in an elegant flat in Brighton, her future secure; Angelica herself had a tiny but very valuable mews cottage, tucked away from view in one of London's precious and increasingly rare oases of peace and quiet. All of the mews houses had separate garages, and the mews itself had no vehicular access to the pretty cobbled courtyard they all shared.

On admittedly rare warm summer weekends, it was not unusual to see all its inhabitants breakfasting al fresco in the courtyard in a manner more reminiscent of France than Britain, on delicacies supplied by a local delicatessen.

It had been on one such morning that she had first met Giles. He had been living in one of the cottages on a temporary basis. He had told her that he had been loaned it by some friends who were spending six months in the States.

Later she had discovered that this was not the truth; that in fact the house belonged to the parents of his previous girlfriend, and that he had casually moved in and refused to move out, claiming the property as his by virtue of his relationship with their daughter.

Giles had had a gift for distorting the truth, for
bending it to suit his own selfish purposes, and she,
like the fool she was, had been completely taken in
by him.

It didn't help that her friends had been equally easily
deceived, that they had been equally stunned by the
truth. They had quickly and determinedly rallied
around her when the blows had fallen, not singly, but
in a massed attack which had left her feeling as though
her heart and her mind had been beaten to a jelly that
made it impossible for her to rationalise herself out
of her anguish and suffering.

And yet she had been so lucky... so very lucky. If
her mother hadn't broken her arm just before she and
Giles were due to take that holiday in Provence, if
she hadn't returned unexpectedly to London that
evening to collect some papers she had needed... If
Giles hadn't been arrogant and reckless enough to
spend not just the evening but the night as well with
someone else, and if she hadn't seen that someone
else leaving his house in the early hours of the
morning, she might never have discovered the truth—
or at least she might only have discovered it when it
was too late.

And the worst of it was that to her own mind at
least she had been so trusting, so idiotic, that she had
actually believed that he loved her, that she had never
questioned why such a charming and good-looking
man of twenty-seven should actually want a woman
like her—a woman who had never really had time to
play and enjoy life, a woman who had dedicated
herself to her business life, a woman who took her

responsibilities so seriously that they were the prime focus of her whole life.

She had been a fool. And it didn't help knowing that she was far from the first woman Giles had deceived. Indeed he had made quite a career out of it, safe in the knowledge that his other victims, like her, would not want to broadcast their idiocy.

It made it no better knowing that she had willingly allowed him to dictate the course of their relationship, to sweep her off her feet, insisting that he loved her, that he wanted to spend the rest of his life with her. That holiday in Provence had been going to be a time of pre-wedding intimacy, a whole month of getting to know one another, of becoming lovers, of committing themselves to their shared future.

She had been so blinded by wonder, by the thrill of believing that he loved her, that she hadn't even looked for any flaws in him.

Tom had told her gently that she mustn't blame herself; that there came a time in everyone's life when they were vulnerable to that kind of foolishness—that she had been lucky because fate had stepped in and saved her before it was too late.

As her solicitor he had felt bound to point out to her that, had she and Giles actually been married, she could have suffered far more than the emotional destruction of her life. She could have virtually lost if not everything she had worked for then certainly a good part of it.

That had been a bitter pill to swallow: the knowledge that Giles, simply because of her imagined wealth, had callously and cold-bloodedly set out to deceive her into believing he loved her. He had wanted, not her, but the company. His desire had not been for her, but for money.

The humiliation of that knowledge was something she thought she would have to carry for the rest of her life—that and the knowledge that she had been such a fool. Falling in love with a cheat was something a girl in her teens could be forgiven, but a woman of her age ought to have known better, ought to have realised... What? That it was impossible for a man to fall instantly and completely in love with someone like her, a woman who, while passably attractive, had hardly the kind of head-turning looks that had men falling over themselves for her attention.

Even now she still couldn't understand why it had happened—why she had so easily allowed herself to be deceived. She shivered suddenly, her flesh going cold as she dwelt on all she had put at risk—not just her own future, but her mother's as well and those of her employees, and all for what? For the meaningless smiles and even more meaningless flattery of a man who had cold-bloodedly set out to use her.

Was she so emotionally bereft of inner strength, so vulnerable, so in need of believing herself loved that she had not had the sense to see what Giles really wanted? Was she so much of an emotional fool that she had really believed him when he'd sworn he loved her, when he'd told her he wanted her as his wife? Why *hadn't* she questioned him more deeply? Why hadn't she suspected?

Because it had never occurred to her that she might fall into that kind of trap, that a man might want her simply because of the financial gain she represented.

That was what hurt her the most of all, she recognised: that she had been stupid enough to believe herself loved when all the time Giles had been laughing at her gullibility, when he had been secretly assessing her financial worth. All those lies about wanting their lovemaking to be perfect, about wanting to take her away somewhere where he could have her all to himself. All those lies, which she had believed, when the truth was that he had already been sleeping with someone else.

In New York women employed private detectives to search into the lives of their menfriends. She had thought them cynical and cold-blooded. Now she was not so sure.

Facing up to the knowledge that she had made such a fool of herself had been the hardest thing she had ever had to do. She had been remorseless with herself, not allowing herself to hide from the truth, making herself confront her own frailties, her own stupidity, making herself see that she had craved being loved so much that she had almost eagerly thrown away her intelligence and self-respect.

Up until Giles's arrival in her life, she had considered herself to be fulfilled and as reasonably happy as any human being could expect to be.

Marriage, children—these were secret dreams she had kept tucked away in a private corner of her mind. She had looked around at the relationships of her friends, seen how very difficult it was in this frenetically paced age merely to find the time to devote to developing and then cosseting emotional bonds, and had told herself prosaically that maybe later in her life she would opt for a sensible, unpassionate marriage to some kind, bland man who would share her desire for children and stability, but that that time had not come yet and that she was presently more than content with her life, that the wild love-affairs indulged in by some of her friends were not for her and more to be looked upon with mild amusement than envy, that the trauma of intense emotional relationships were never worth the expenditure of time and emotion that went into them.

And then she had met Giles, and he had turned her whole world upside-down, and she, fool that she was, had helped him.

Well, she was suffering for that self-indulgence now.

'Exhaustion' was her doctor's pithy diagnosis of the enervating malaise that had drained her to the point where she felt she could simply no longer function as the person she had once been.

There had been a good deal of shocked reaction from her friends. The words 'yuppie flu' had floated sympathetically on the air. None of them had been tactless enough to suggest she was suffering from something as unfashionable as the misery caused by a broken heart, especially as it was twelve months since she and Giles had parted. Modern women did not have hearts that broke; they were far too sensible, far too mature. They wisely assessed the advantages and disadvantages of every relationship they entered, not having the time to waste on those that were unprofitable. If only she had followed that sensible course...But she hadn't, had she? And she was left, not only with the pain of being deceived by someone she had thought cared for her, not only with the anguish of her own misery and her bruised pride, but she was also having to contend with the realisation that she was not the woman she had always supposed; that she was not the mature, wise creature she had always prided herself on being; that she was in fact as vulnerable as the rest of her sex when it came to her deepest emotions and needs.

Which was why, on the insistence of her doctor, she was taking this enforced break. It had been Tom, her solicitor, and one of her closest friends, who had offered her the use of the Pembrokeshire cottage he had recently inherited from an uncle.

'It's virtually in the middle of nowhere, five miles from the nearest village, but the countryside is wonderful. I went down there never having even seen the place. I'd already made up my mind to sell, but once I did see it... Well, I've decided to keep it, and it's yours for just as long as you need it, Angelica.'

She had wanted to protest that she wasn't an invalid, that she didn't need it, that she didn't need anything or anyone; that was how raw and sore she still was inside, but she had known she would have been lying. She badly needed somewhere to crawl away into and hide, somewhere where she could lick her wounds and recover at her own pace.

She could leave the business in the capable hands of Paul Lyons, her second-in-command; she knew that.

She didn't love Giles any more. How could she? The man she had thought she loved had never actually existed, but that didn't stop her heart from thumping crazily every time she saw a man with fair, sun-streaked hair and blue eyes. It didn't stop her from waking up alone at night with her face stiff from the drying salt of her tears. It didn't stop her from feeling it was impossible for her to face the world, from feeling that everyone who looked at her knew what a fool she had been.

Tom was right—six weeks away from London, living simply and on her own, was probably just what she needed to get things back into perspective, to recoup her old energy and determination.

They had had lunch together yesterday, and then he had gone back to the house with her, to make sure that she had got the route clear, he had said, but she had known that he was worried about her. That knowledge had warmed her. She and Tom had been friends for a long time. Her mother adored him, and often hinted that they would make a good couple, but, close though they were, both of them had separately and mutually acknowledged that their relationship was more akin to one of brother and sister, that their emotional bonding was such that it precluded any possibility of sexual desire. Tom had recently fallen in love, and she liked his new girlfriend very much.

She had broken her journey in Ludlow to admire the pretty town and have something to eat, and had perhaps, she recognised, lingered there rather longer than was wise, because now it was dark; the country road was unlit, and she was glad of the absence of any other traffic, otherwise she suspected she would have irritated the other drivers by her hesitancy as she searched the roadside for the turn-off for the cottage.

She was becoming increasingly anxious to find it, not just because it was late and she was tired; for the last few miles she had been feeling increasingly unwell.

Her stomach hurt, she felt sick, and she was pretty sure that the meal she had eaten in Ludlow was to blame.

She had lost almost a stone in the twelve months since she had parted from Giles. Her friends were beginning to warn her that there was such a thing as becoming too slender, and that her five-foot-seven frame was beginning to look a touch gaunt. She had been forced to acknowledge the truth of their remarks. She could see new hollows at the base of her throat, could feel a new prominence in the bones of her hips, a new slackness in the waists of her discreetly elegant skirts. There were shadows beneath her eyes turning them from grey to haunted violet, the soft black silkiness of her hair was beginning to lose its gloss, and she knew that the emotional devastation she had suffered was beginning to show its physical signs on her body.

She had promised herself that she would spend this break getting herself fit; walking, eating sensibly, living simply and wholesomely instead of picking reluctantly at meals she never seemed to finish and keeping herself closeted in the unhealthy stuffiness of her centrally heated office.

The cottage was spartan, Tom had warned her, but they were having a good summer, and she had felt a sharp relief at the prospect of living alone somewhere where no one would expect her to make any effort to keep up the appearance of the glossy, self-sufficient career woman.

That was the trouble with being a woman, she reflected muzzily; nature had not designed them to be self-sufficient. Nature had ensured that they would always inherit those genes which made them yearn to share and nurture. Nature was a fool and a cheat—just like Giles—and she was a bigger fool for having allowed herself to be deceived.

Too late she saw the turning and had to reverse the car. Doing so made her feel horribly faint and sick. Her head felt as though it were stuffed with cotton wool, while her stomach...

As she drove down the lane between high, hedge-topped banks, she prayed that she would make it to the cottage before her stomach rebelled completely.

She could feel sweat breaking out on her skin, the kind of sweat that heralded a bout of sickness, and then mercifully as she turned a corner the car's head-lights picked out the low stone-built cottage. Longer than she had expected, and was her brain playing tricks on her or did it seem as though it had two sep-arate front doors, and what was that hedge doing in the middle of the front garden?

As she stopped the car, she realised muzzily that it wasn't one cottage but a pair of semis, in fact. She just had time to realise that Tom hadn't warned her that the cottage didn't stand completely alone before violent cramps seized her stomach.

Throwing open the car door, she virtually fell out of the driver's seat, and was immediately and vi-olently ill.

Shivering and shaking, her body doubled up with the intensity of the violent spasms racking her stomach, she prayed they would abate for long enough for her to make it to the privacy of the cottage. Not that there was anyone to see her. No lights shone from the windows of either cottage, no sound apart from the chattering of her own teeth spoiled the perfect silence. She was alone—completely alone ...

Tensely she straightened up, relieved to discover that, while she felt appallingly weak, the pain and nausea had faded—at least for the time being.

Hurrying back to the car, she extracted her bag, and found the large, old-fashioned key to the cottage. Not bothering to lock her car, she opened the wooden gate and hurried down the path to the front door.

The effort of trying to control the pain in her stomach was making her feel positively light-headed, she acknowledged as she tried shakily to insert the key in the lock. A horrible sense of weakness overwhelmed her, the return of the unbearable cramping agony in her stomach bringing a film of sweat to her forehead, and nausea burning in her throat.

As the pain increased, she dropped the key, gripping her stomach, all her concentration demanded by the intensity of her agony.

As she cried out, and half collapsed on to the ground in front of the cottage, she was dimly conscious of a car engine fading into silence somewhere in the distance, but she was far too occupied with her own physical needs to pay it much attention.

She had just finished being violently sick, tears of pain and shock pouring down her face, her throat raw with the violence of her retching, her body still huddled on the ground, as she fought against the dizzying waves of agony beginning to build up inside her again when she heard an irritated male voice demanding from behind her, 'What the devil's going on?'

And then as she tried to turn her head, too exhausted and in too much pain to question either the man's arrival or his anger, he obviously realised for himself how ill she was, because he made a sudden sound of enlightenment and then crouched down beside her, saying in a much kinder tone, 'It's all right. No, don't try to move. What happened? Food poisoning?'

The cramping pains were increasing again. Angelica only had time to nod before they became so violent that she stopped fighting to stay conscious and let herself slide down into the waiting darkness, vaguely conscious of someone lifting her, carrying her, speaking to her before the darkness completely closed over her.

CHAPTER TWO

RELUCTANTLY Angelica opened her eyes, wincing as the light hit them, and closing them again, the mere effort of turning her head in the direction of the light so exhausting that it drained her.

She felt oddly light-headed . . . empty and fragile. She had a collection of hazy memories and impressions, the sharpest of them being a pain so intense that even to remember it made her stomach muscles tense defensively.

She had been sick, more violently sick than she could ever remember being in her life. So sick and in so much pain that she had honestly thought she was going to die—had even at times wished that she might . . .

She remembered saying as much, and she remembered another unfamiliar voice cautioning her against such folly, calming and soothing her, just as unfamiliar hands had dealt with the physical agony of her illness.

Who had they belonged to, those hands and that voice? A doctor? Her forehead crinkled in a frown as she tried to analyse why she should reject that thought so rigorously. Not a doctor, then who?

A stranger almost certainly, and yet oddly she had found the fact that he was a stranger comforting rather than intimidating, as though had she known him in some way she would have been obliged to put up a

pretence of not needing the assistance he was giving
her, instead of sinking weakly and gratefully into his
care, allowing him all manner of intimacies with her
pain-racked flesh that would have been intolerable had
she actually known the owner of those capable, clinical
hands and that calming, knowing voice that somehow
assured her that he knew exactly what she was en-
during, how much it frightened her, how vulnerable
and weak it made her... How little she wanted to be
beholden to him or anyone else.

Her mind felt cloudy and confused; the more she
tried to focus it, the more woolly her thoughts became.
She didn't even know where she was...

But, yes, she did—she was in Wales—
Pembrokeshire. She had come here to rest... Her
mouth twisted slightly. Surely only *she* could start off
what was supposed to be a period of complete rest
and recuperation with a bout of food poisoning so
intense that her memories of the last few days were
no more than vague wisps of uncertain flashes of
reality mingled with long periods of cloudy uncertainty, the whole time sharply delineated by her memories of the agony of her illness.

She remembered arriving at the cottage, and that
must be where she was now, surely? This bedroom
with its sloping eaves and its view of the distant hills;
this old-fashioned, iron-framed bed, so high off the
ground that it was impossible for her feet to touch
the floor.

She frowned. How did she know that? She had a
vague memory of desperately wanting to be sick, of
trying to clamber out of the high bed and find the

bathroom, only to be stopped, and then firmly carried there . . .

Strange how, in recollecting the incident, she should feel consumed with the very natural embarrassment she could quite clearly remember she had not felt at the time. Almost as though somehow he, whoever he was, had been so clinical and detached, so assured and firm in his handling of the situation and of her that she had felt nothing other than an exhausted desire to simply give in and let him take control.

It shocked her to realise that she had shared an intimacy with this stranger that she had never shared with Giles. Not the intimacy of lovers of course, but an intimacy which in its way made her feel even more vulnerable. And yet she had not felt vulnerable at the time...had not felt anything other than a weak, shaky gratitude. She even remembered now trying to thank him at some stage, but he had brushed her thanks aside. Where was he now? Had he gone? Left her alone?

For some reason that thought panicked her. Without thinking what she was doing she pushed back the quilt and the heavy linen sheet, swinging her legs to the floor, and discovering as she did so that she had been quite correct in remembering that the bed was too high for her to reach the floor, and also that, instead of one of her own long, sensible nightdresses, she seemed to be wearing a man's shirt.

A man's shirt with just enough buttons fastened for decency, as though whoever had fastened her into it had known that when she woke up she would remember the intimacies they had shared, and who had taken pains to reassure her that, no matter what he might have done to help her in the extremity of her need, he both understood and respected her desire to recover her privacy. As though he was reassuring her that there had been nothing voyeuristic or lustful in his intimacy with her flesh. As though he had known how shocked she would be when she remembered how he had helped her, carried her, bathed her.

Her body suddenly grew hot, her face flushing. She didn't want to remember anything like that. He had helped her and she was grateful to him, whoever he was, but now that she was herself again . . .

She slid her feet on to the floor and stood up, or rather she tried to stand up, her eyes widening in surprise and disbelief as her legs refused to support her.

As she crumpled to the floor, she only just had time to grab hold of the side of the bed.

The next thing she knew the bedroom door was being flung open and a man strode in, limping slightly as he made his way to the bed. He was frowning down at her, his dark hair damp and untidy as though he had just been towelling it dry, his jaw shadowed with an overnight growth of beard. The jeans he was wearing seemed a little loose on the waist and the hips, as though he had recently lost weight.

When he bent down to help her she caught the scent of his soap, clean and masculine, and realised that he must have been in the bathroom.

'It's all right. I can manage,' she told him self-consciously, trying to pull away from him as he picked her up bodily, depositing her back on the bed.

The look he gave her spoke volumes and made her flush guiltily. She owed him far too large a debt of gratitude already without compounding that debt.

It seemed unfair that fate should have decreed that this should happen to her just when she had made up her mind that henceforth she would live her life as independently and free from emotional commitment as she could.

But all men weren't like Giles. There was Tom, for instance, who had been such a good friend to her over the years. Tom, and Paul, her second-in-command at the factory, both of whom she trusted implicitly, both of whom had proved their friendship and affection for her.

But then that was the difference between her relationship with them and the disastrous relationship she had had with Giles. They were friends—not potential lovers.

Perhaps she was the kind of woman who was safer establishing non-sexual relationships with men. The sort of woman who aroused affection in the male breast rather than adoration.

She realised abruptly that the hard arms imprisoning her had been removed, and that the owner of those arms was now leaning over her still frowning down at her.

He had nice arms, she reflected absently, firm and well muscled without being in any way over-developed. His skin was weather-beaten rather than tanned, as though he worked outside.

For the first time she was curious about him... About how on earth he had materialised so fortuitously in her time of need. About what he was doing in the first place in such a remote spot. About where he ought to have been rather than here, taking care of her.

'You still aren't well enough to get up,' he told her firmly.

He had a pleasant voice, deep and faintly husky, but with no marked Welsh accent.

'I'm feeling much better,' Angelica protested. 'I really ought to get up. I've taken up far too much of your time as it is.' Her skin went faintly pink as she added uncertainly, 'You really were a Good Samaritan. If you hadn't arrived when you did...' She gave a tiny shiver, not wanting to dwell on what might have happened to her. 'I had no idea there were two cottages here,' she told him as he slowly straightened up. 'When Tom described this place to me he omitted to mention the fact that it was one of a pair of semis.'

She watched as his eyebrows rose a little, and for some reason felt obliged to add defensively, 'Not that I'm not thankful to you for all that you've done, but I can't impose on you any longer. You must have things of your own to do—your own cottage to——'

'This *is* my cottage,' he told her blandly, and when her mouth dropped a little he added coolly, 'When I found you virtually out cold on my doorstep, I'd no idea who you were or what you were doing here and it seemed better to take you inside with me rather than wait for you to come round to find out. When I got the doctor out from Aberystwyth it was touch and go for the first twenty-four hours whether or not he'd have to find you a bed in our one and only local hospital.

'By the time we'd managed to find out who you were and what you were doing here, it seemed easier from my point of view to keep an eye on you here than to move you next door.'

He said it all so matter-of-factly that Angelica could do nothing other than smile uncomfortably at him and say weakly, 'I've put you to a good deal of trouble. I'm so sorry.'

'No need to be. Being ill is no picnic. I know—I've been there myself. There are times when we all need a little help.'

Angelica frowned. What did he mean, he'd been there himself? Now that she looked properly at him, she saw that there was a gauntness about his face, a sharpness around those high sculpted cheekbones, narrow grooves cut either side of his mouth that hinted at pain and suffering.

She remembered how he'd limped when he walked into the bedroom and was suddenly and totally unexpectedly curious about him. And then she realised what he had said about the cottage. This wasn't Tom's cottage—it was his.

'Look, I feel dreadful about all of this,' she told him truthfully. 'I must have caused you a great deal of trouble, but I'm over it now, and perfectly well enough to move into Tom's cottage. I feel I've trespassed on your privacy for long enough.'

'You aren't going anywhere until the doctor says you can,' he told her flatly.

Angelica eyed him uncertainly. There was nothing threatening in his attitude, nothing aggressive or domineering, and yet she had the inner impression that if she tried to defy him, if she tried to get up and physically remove herself from his presence, she would very soon find herself right back in this bed.

It startled her how very easy she found it to submit to the strength she could feel emanating from him; almost as though she was *relieved* to be able to do so, to let him make her decisions for her.

She shivered slightly, remembering how her own doctor had warned her that the stress she had been under could manifest itself in many different ways. Was this another of them—this reluctance to take charge of her own life, this unfamiliar desire to simply lie here and let this man, this stranger, make her decisions for her?

She shivered again, suddenly conscious of how much her relationship with Giles had changed her, how much it had undermined her self-confidence, and, although she was mercifully free of any shadow of the love she had once thought she felt for him, she was left with this weak indecisiveness, this inability to trust her own judgement, to make up her own mind, in a way that was completely at odds with the woman she had always thought herself to be.

'Something wrong?' enquired her rescuer.

The abrupt question startled her. She shook her head, a little nervous of his perception, wondering what he might have read in her unguarded expression.

'Have you owned your cottage long?' she asked him quickly, trying to redirect their conversation into less emotive and personal channels.

He stood up and told her curtly, 'I don't own it. I'm renting it.'

It was Angelica's turn to frown. His words were innocuous enough and certainly there was no real reason for the warning bells to ring so loudly in her ears. But Angelica had been running her own business and dealing with people for long enough to recognise 'keep off' signs when they were posted. She had after all been posting enough of her own recently to be instantly aware of when she had trespassed on to forbidden ground. And yet what could there have been in her innocent enquiry about his ownership of the cottage to draw that curt, rejecting response that warned her it was a not a subject he wished to pursue?

Shrugging mentally, she told herself that it was no real business of hers. She wasn't particularly interested in whether or not he owned the cottage anyway. She had only been trying to make conversation.

And yet... And yet...as he stood there with his back to her, the muscles in his shoulders and back so obviously stiff with tension and anger, she felt a totally unexpected surge of sensation, not strong enough to be an actual emotional pain, and yet certainly strong enough to be rather more than conventional pique.

She trembled a little, hugging her arms around her body, not liking the idea that the physical intimacy forced on her by her illness had somehow or other forged within her mind, albeit unconsciously, the right to feel affronted and hurt by his obvious desire to shut her out.

As he stood there he shifted his weight from one foot to the other, his palm absently rubbing the muscle in one thigh as though it was causing him pain.

'I've been in touch with your friend Tom, by the way,' he told her, turning back to her.

'You've been in touch with Tom? You know him, then?'

She was puzzled, confused that Tom had not mentioned this neighbour.

'No. We've never met, but you had his telephone number scribbled down on your map.'

Angelica nodded. Tom, bless him, had taken the precaution of jotting down his new London telephone number just in case she couldn't follow his directions. He had moved house a fortnight ago and she had not as yet memorised his new telephone number.

'I didn't ring him until after the doctor had confirmed that you were suffering from salmonella. He wanted to drive down here to be with you, but it seems he had other commitments.'

'Yes,' Angelica agreed with a smile that was fond and more betraying than she knew. 'He was going to spend the weekend with his new girlfriend's parents. It's the first time they've met and since he suspects that they're a little concerned at the age gap between them—Tom's thirty-two and Sarah is only nineteen, although a very mature nineteen—I know he wouldn't have wanted to put them off. Nor would I have wanted him to. In fact, grateful though I am to you, *you* really shouldn't have burdened yourself with me. Surely a private nurse . . .?'

His eyebrows rose. 'Maybe, but they are not easy to come by in this part of the world, especially at such short notice. Your Tom warned me that I was going to have trouble with you once you were over the worst. A very independent lady was how he described you . . .'

A very independent lady. She had been once and had prided herself on it. Now she wasn't so sure, and neither, she knew, was Tom. But, bless him, like the good friend he was, he would have taken care not to betray her vulnerabilities to anyone else.

'What time is the doctor due?' she asked quietly. She had imposed on this man for long enough. The intimacies that had passed between them while she was incapable of looking after herself were something she had to accept, and yet now, confronted with the reality of a man who before had simply been a shadowy, unfamiliar figure, a gentle, capable pair of hands that seemed to know instinctively how to help and soothe, a calm, understanding voice, she was beginning to feel acutely self-conscious and vulnerable.

The look he gave her seemed to slice right through her defences and fasten on all that she was feeling. He had coldly clear pale blue eyes that in some lights looked almost grey; dangerously seeing eyes, she recognised uncomfortably, that went well with what she was beginning to suspect was an equally perceptive mind.

She wondered obliquely what he did for a living. There was no obvious industry in this part of the world; it was an idyllic spot for holiday-makers, for those in search of solitude and peace, but for those who lived locally... And what kind of work allowed a man to take days off without any notice, to nurse a complete stranger? Did he in fact work at all, or was he perhaps one of that breed of people she had occasionally read about and puzzled over but never met: a genuine drop-out from society?

She eyed him covertly, registering the well-worn jeans, the slightly too thin frame. If he didn't work how did he manage to pay the rent on this place? How did he feed and clothe himself?

'I can hear a car outside,' he told her. 'It will probably be the doctor now. I'd better go down and let him in.'

His hearing was as acute as his perception, Angelica recognised as she too heard the approaching sound of a car engine.

The doctor, when he came into the bedroom, proved to be a middle-aged man with a soft Welsh accent and tired eyes. When Angelica apologised for causing him so much trouble, he shook his head and told her, 'There's nothing worse than a nasty bout of food poisoning. You were lucky that Daniel was here when you collapsed.'

'Very lucky,' Angelica agreed hollowly, shivering a little as she remembered her physical agony and distress when she first became ill. So his name was Daniel. Foolish of her not to have asked him herself.

'Your friend gave us the name of your London doctor.' The shrewd, tired eyes studied her. 'Come down here for a bit of a rest, have you?'

Angelica pulled a face. 'He says I'm suffering from stress. When Tom offered me the use of his cottage...'

'Stress, is it? Well, then, you'll be needing a bit of peace and quiet.'

'Yes,' Angelica agreed. 'I feel I ought to move into Tom's cottage and let Mr—er—Daniel get on with his own life.'

For some reason she could feel her face growing hot as she spoke, as much because of the thoughtful way the doctor was studying her as because of her discomfort at not even knowing her rescuer's name.

'I feel very guilty about the way I've been taking up his time,' she added awkwardly. 'I did think that perhaps a nurse—— '

'There's not much Daniel doesn't know about what it's like to be ill,' she was told calmly. 'And as for taking up his time, well, I dare say if he hadn't wanted to help you he'd soon have made some other arrangements, although out here people do tend to take it for granted that neighbours will help one another out.'

The doctor was standing up, his examination finished. 'You'll be feeling very weak for a few days yet,' he warned her.

'But I can get up,' Angelica pressed. She had already made up her mind that she simply could not impose on her host any longer. And besides, now that she was properly conscious, properly aware, well, she felt both uncomfortable and guilty about the way she had been so dependent on Daniel. Dependency wasn't something she was used to, and since the débâcle of her relationship with Giles she had striven very hard to regain her former self-reliance. It had become very important to her that she was independent of other people, that she was able to function completely on her resources. She was never, ever again going to allow herself to suffer the kind of emotional trauma and pain she had suffered with Giles.

'Yes, you can get up,' the doctor agreed, frowning thoughtfully at her, 'but I must warn you against trying to do too much too soon. You could very easily have a relapse. Salmonella is never something to be treated lightly and when it's as severe as this bout

you've just had...' His frown deepened, and Angelica
had the feeling that he was about to say something
else, but obviously he must have changed his mind
because after a few seconds' pause he smiled at her
and said kindly, 'This isn't London, you know. Here
we take our responsibility to our small communities
and to each other very seriously indeed. You mustn't
feel guilty about needing Daniel's help. Just think of
it as a good deed you've been "loaned", and which
one day you'll have the opportunity to pass on to
someone else.'

He gave her another smile, closed his bag and
headed for the door before she could say anything
else.

Angelica heard Daniel talking to him when he went
downstairs, and sensitively wondered if it was her they
were discussing. It was stupid to feel so vulnerable,
so defensive, she chided herself.

Surely she was mature enough, sensible enough to
realise that all men weren't like Giles—that she had
been unlucky and perhaps a little foolish, but that the
pain she had suffered was no reason to turn her back
on the entire male sex, mistrustful and afraid of every
single one of its members.

Maybe not, but it would be folly to allow herself
to fall in love again, to——

Fall in love? She frowned heavily. Who on earth
was talking about falling in love, for heaven's sake?
What possible link could there be between her relationship with Giles and the very, very different relationship which circumstances had forced on her with
Daniel?

Daniel. She tasted the name, testing it cautiously, acknowledging that in some way it suited him. It was a powerful name, a little awesome in some ways. Like the man himself? *Did* she find him powerful and just a little intimidating? Just a little bit too much the dominant male animal, supremely confident of himself, in a way she knew she could never be?

Was it an inbuilt flaw of her sex that it was so constantly vulnerable, so constantly aware of its failings and insecurities? Wasn't it because of her own awareness of her personal, deep-rooted insecurities, her fear that her life was starting to revolve too completely around her work that she had been so dangerously open to Giles's deliberate manipulation? Had she had a stronger, tougher, more male-based personality, she would have been too self-sufficient, too sure of herself and confident to fall for Giles's rather obvious and facile charm.

Was she never going to stop feeling guilty for being such a fool, for not realising far sooner than she had just what Giles was? It still galled her to realise that, in the eyes of others, she must have seemed both stupid and laughable; a mature woman, so desperately craving love and reassurance that she had not been able to see the truth.

She was never going to allow herself to be deceived like that again. From now on her relationships with men were going to be strictly non-emotional, strictly held at a safe distance from her too vulnerable heart.

It still tore at her emotionally that, despite the success she had made of her business life, she still felt this emptiness, this yearning, this need to be fulfilled as a woman.

She shivered a little, all too well able to imagine how the man downstairs would laugh at that kind of vulnerability. Even Tom, great friend though he was, had not really understood this deep-rooted need she had to love and be loved in return. At times she didn't even understand it herself, resenting its hold on her, wishing there was some way she could destroy it so that it never made her vulnerable again.

If she couldn't destroy her own inner need, then at least she could ensure that no man ever got close enough to use it against her, manipulating her, deceiving her.

She moved restlessly, conscious of a sharp, biting anger that fate had decreed that she should be rendered so helpless and vulnerable that she had had no option but to accept Daniel's help.

Why couldn't it have been another *woman* who had found her there on the doorstep? Why did it have to be an unknown *man*—a man, moreover, who, despite his shabby clothes and generally down-at-heel appearance, seemed to exude power and strength in a way that only seemed to reinforce her own appalling weakness?

Despite what the doctor had said, despite his warnings, the sooner she moved into Tom's cottage and away from Daniel, the better.

She said as much to Daniel himself half an hour later when he came upstairs, glibly omitting to tell him that while the doctor had said she might get up he had also warned her against overdoing things.

'I really do feel I've trespassed on your time and hospitality far too long,' she told him coolly, adopting her most businesslike manner and trying not to feel acutely conscious of the fact that all she was wearing was one of his shirts. 'And the doctor agrees with me that I am now well enough to manage on my own.'

Was there just a suspicion of a betraying tremor in her voice as she spoke this small fib? Was she tilting her chin just a little too much as though defying him to argue with her, and, when he didn't, when he simply continued to regard her thoughtfully, was that really a tiny thread of disappointment that tangled with her relief, increasing her anxiety to escape to the security and privacy of Tom's cottage?

'If you're sure you can manage,' he said at last.

'Yes. Yes, I am,' and then, aware that it might seem as though she was not aware of all that he had done for her, she added quickly, 'I'm very grateful to you of course, and if there's anything I can do to repay you . . .'

The smile he gave her almost seemed to mock her as though he knew exactly how desperate she was to escape from him.

'I still don't even know your name,' she told him fretfully, hating the way she felt at such a disadvantage. Now that she was fully conscious again, she was acutely aware of her unmade-up face and tousled hair, her borrowed and unconventional nightshirt, while he stood watching her armoured in the secure protection of his jeans and shirt. Now when it was the last thing she wanted to do, she had a series of illuminating and embarrassing mental memories of hazy moments of consciousness when she had called out for help, and he had been there, his hands holding her, soothing her, his movements calm and sure as though he had known instinctively what to do.

No nurse however professional could have cared for her so conscientiously. She was overwhelmingly grateful to him, and at the same time she was intensely self-conscious and embarrassed about the intimacies which had passed between them; intimacies which, even if she had been only half conscious at the time and in no fit state to do anything other than submit thankfully to his care, had remained uncomfortably sharply etched in her memory.

She remembered after one particularly gruelling bout of sickness how he had stripped off her clothes, and gently sponged her skin, almost seeming to know how intensely she longed to feel the clean coolness of fresh water on her body washing away the smell and heat of her nausea.

Looking at him now, it seemed impossible that he had shown such care, such . . . such tenderness. She felt her face grow hot with guilt and anger. What was the matter with her? He had simply done what he had felt necessary. In this part of the world neighbours helped one another, the doctor had told her that. There was no reason for her to feel so intensely aware of him—so intensely aware of him in fact that it was as though her flesh had somehow memorised the touch of his hands to such an extent that it now——

She swallowed hard, reining in her runaway thoughts, and almost blurted out, 'I *can't* stay here any longer.'

She saw the way his eyebrows drew together, and bit her lip. What on earth was the matter with her? She was behaving like a fool. Like a woman suddenly terrified of intimacy with a man for whom she felt a dangerous sexual awareness, and there was nothing like that about this situation.

There had been *nothing* remotely sexual in the way he had helped her. There was nothing in his manner now to indicate any degree of sexual awareness of her as a woman. No, the awareness was all on her side, she acknowledged bitterly. And yet why should she be aware of him? He wasn't good-looking in the fair-haired, smooth way which Giles had been. He was too rugged, too roughly hewn, too powerfully male to have that kind of appeal. And even if there was nothing outwardly aggressively sexual about him, she had an instinctive knowledge that he was the kind of man that women would find strongly sexual. Not the kind of man who appealed to her at all. *She* had always avoided that particular type, finding them slightly intimidating, and they had normally avoided her, obviously realising that she was not the intensely sexually responsive type.

It was her relationship with Giles that had left her so vulnerable, so bruised and so lacking in self-worth that she had become acutely conscious of this man *as* a man. When he took a step towards her she found she was actually trembling. He saw it and frowned.

'You're still too weak to get up yet,' he told her curtly. 'You'll stay here tonight and then in the morning, if you're feeling up to it, we'll see about getting you moved into the other cottage.'

She ought to have objected, to have told him that *she* was the one making the decisions, that it was *her* right to make them, that she was an adult woman and had no intentions of allowing him to dictate to her in any way, but she was still trembling inside, still desperately conscious of the fact that she wished he would move away from her.

'I came up to see if you could manage some home-made broth,' he told her, changing the subject.

Home-made broth. She stared at him as though he read her mind; he gave her a brief smile and told her, 'No, I haven't made it myself. The farmer's wife gave it to me when I went to get the milk and eggs. She'd heard that you weren't well.'

'The farm—is it far?' Angelica asked him.

'Not really; a couple of miles, that's all. I walk over every other day or so.'

A couple of miles. She swallowed hard. In London the furthest she ever walked was a hundred yards or so. The thought of walking a couple of miles in her present condition made her all too glad that she had her car. And then, without meaning to do so, she glanced automatically at Daniel's lame leg.

'The exercise is good for it,' he told her curtly, so obviously following her train of thought that she flushed with guilt and embarrassment.

'I'm sorry,' she apologised. 'I was just——'

'You were wondering how I managed to walk that far,' Daniel supplied carelessly for her. 'It wasn't easy at first, but it's like everything else: something you eventually get used to. It helps to strengthen the damaged muscles—or so they tell me.'

Was that bitterness she could hear underlying the harsh words? She wondered what had caused his lameness. Had he been injured in an accident? She found herself shivering at the thought and then was angry with herself for being so concerned. What business was it of hers *what* had happened to him?

'Well?' Daniel prompted, while she battled with her wayward emotions, and stared at him in confusion. 'The broth,' he reminded her. '*Would* you like some? Mrs Davies has sent some of her home-made bread as well. I've got an Aga here in the kitchen and I've been trying my hand at baking some, but I must add as yet I haven't had any success.'

He'd been trying *his* hand at baking bread. Angelica gulped as she stared at him.

'We have some bad storms on this coast,' he told her wryly. 'It's possible to be cut off here, even from the farm, for days at a time. Self-sufficiency here isn't an affectation, it's a necessity, and if the power goes off—which it can do—the Aga is the only source of heat.

'Your friend would be as well to get one installed in his place, especially if he intends to use it during the winter.'

'I'll tell him,' Angelica responded. 'And, yes, I would like some broth please.'

'Good. In that case, I think we'll get you downstairs, and just see how strong you do feel once you're on your feet.'

At the same moment as Angelica swung her feet to the floor, he walked towards her, closing the gap between them and picking her up before she could draw breath to protest.

His shirt rode up to reveal the pale slenderness of her thighs, and, although she knew he had carried her like this on a dozen or more previous occasions, now that she was fully conscious she was acutely aware of the intimacy of his hold, of the strength and the heat radiating from his flesh where it touched her, of the way she had to lean against him so that her head was tucked into his shoulder, her breast pushing softly against his chest, one arm underneath her as he supported her, the other holding her tightly, so that she had no alternative but to lock her own arms around his neck even while she protested.

'Please—I can walk.'

'You mean you *think* you can,' he derided her. 'The last thing we need now is you collapsing and falling downstairs. Let's see how you go on when you're downstairs before we get too adventurous, shall we?'

He really was the limit, Angelica decided wrathfully. Telling her what she could and could not do. Laying down the law, when she was perfectly capable of making her own decisions. If it weren't for the fact that she owed him so much, she would have told him in no uncertain terms that no one dictated to her, that no man was allowed to dominate her life... Not any more. She had learned the dangers of becoming too dependent on a man the hard way, and it was a lesson she intended to keep firmly to the forefront of her mind.

The cottage's stairs were very narrow and Angelica found she was instinctively holding her breath, her arms tightening as Daniel carried her down them.

'It's all right,' he assured her. 'I won't drop you. If I haven't dropped you yet, I don't think you need worry that I'm going to do so now.'

For some reason his words, which she suspected were intended to be reassuring, conjured up such images of intimacy within her too imaginative brain that she found herself trying desperately to arch her body away from him. His heartbeat was faintly erratic as though he was in fact finding her heavier than he pretended.

He might have carried her like this before, but then she had been in no state to register such things as the powerful contraction of his muscles, the warmth of his breath against her skin, the heat of his body, the scent of it stimulating her senses in a way she had never known before, not even with Giles.

To her anguished chagrin, she could actually feel her body reacting to his proximity in a way that made her desperately anxious to be out of his arms.

What was the matter with her? After Giles, she had told herself that never, ever again would she allow herself to be emotionally and sexually involved with a man. It was too dangerous—too painful.

Giles had made her all too acutely aware of how dangerous it was to allow herself to love. She was lucky she had discovered the truth about him before she had committed herself too deeply. As it was she had been hurt, but thankfully not fatally, and with hindsight she could see that her pride had been more bruised than her heart.

Even so it had been a salutary lesson, and one which had made sharply clear to her the dangers of allowing the vulnerable feminine need within her to take control of her life.

'There,' Daniel told her when they reached the bottom of the stairs. 'I told you you'd be quite safe.'

Quite safe. Odd how the words caused a tiny pulse to jump in her throat and her heart to thud warningly.

'If you don't mind, we'll eat in the kitchen. I tend to live in there.'

He nudged open the door with his foot and carried her into the warm, food-scented room, placing her carefully into a comfortable Windsor chair next to the Aga.

CHAPTER THREE

'How's the soup?'

'Wonderful,' Angelica responded truthfully.

She had virtually emptied her bowl, and her stomach felt pleasantly full, although she suspected it would be a few days before she was once more able to digest solid meals.

Loath though she was to admit it, the bout of food poisoning she had suffered had been far more debilitating than she had realised. After less than an hour downstairs, cosseted by the warmth of the Aga, without having to move an inch from her comfortable chair, she was still conscious of a variety of small aches and pains, of a lassitude and exhaustion that warned her that it was not going to be easy to go straight from the luxury of being pampered and cared for by Daniel to the austerity of being alone and looking after herself.

The very fact that she should feel this reluctance, this desire to stay here with him, made it even more imperative that she *did* leave, and the sooner, the better.

Because of that, once she had finished her soup she forced herself to stand up, and before Daniel could stop her she collected both their bowls and carried them over to the sink intending to wash them up.

Daniel's sharp, 'Leave those...' stopped her.

'You've spent the last seventy-two hours in bed,' he told her curtly when she looked at him. 'It's going to be days yet before you get your strength fully back. I don't want you having a relapse.'

'I'm not *going* to have one,' Angelica retaliated sharply. 'Believe me, I'm grateful for all you've done, but all I want to do now is to get back on my own two feet and leave you in peace.'

Something seemed to harden in his eyes as he looked at her. 'Independent, aren't you?'

Her chin tilted. 'Yes, as a matter of fact I am.'

'A career woman with no time for sentiment or weakness.'

He sounded so bitterly angry that she couldn't make any response.

'The kind of woman who thinks nothing matters other than fulfilling her own ambitions.'

His accusation delivered in a harsh, biting voice goaded her into responding.

'And if I am? I suppose *you're* the kind of man who likes his woman helpless and vulnerable.'

She'd gone too far, said too much. The face he turned towards her might have been carved from stone.

'I'm sorry,' she apologised stiltedly. 'You've been very kind to me.'

'Because you were helpless and vulnerable, you mean. Well, for your information——' He broke off, compressing his mouth. 'Convalescence is always harder to cope with than actually being ill. It's hard having to accept the limitations of your own body, especially when you've always been used to full health.'

'Yes,' Angelica agreed starkly. She wanted to apologise for being so quarrelsome, to explain that the reason she was so desperate to get back on her feet was because she was afraid, afraid of becoming too dependent on him. It was as much for his sake as for her own... but she was too proud, too self-conscious to be so open with him. He already knew all the secrets of her body, she could not, dared not, reveal those of her mind to him as well.

Instead she asked uncertainly, 'You've been ill yourself? The doctor told me.'

'Yes.'

He didn't say anything else, busying himself making their coffee, and Angelica knew that, whatever it was that had happened to him, it wasn't something he intended to discuss with her. It was silly for her to feel hurt, shut out, rejected almost, but nevertheless she did, so much so that she had to fight to stop herself saying that she no longer wanted any coffee and that she wanted to go back upstairs. Like a child crying for attention, she acknowledged cynically, but she was long past being allowed the indulgences of childhood and it would be dangerous to allow herself to give in to her foolish need to simply lean on this man and let him become a part of her life.

He had helped her as one neighbour to another, out of necessity and nothing else. This feeling of intimacy, of closeness with him which she was fighting so hard against, must not be something she allowed to grow... Hadn't she learned her lesson with Giles?

Nearly twelve months after Giles's exit from her life she was still suffering the after-effects of his cruelty. That was, after all, why she was here—to give her mind and body time to recover from the strains she had been imposing on them. At the time she had discovered Giles's deceit she had been able to do nothing other than absorb the shock and go on, too involved in negotiating an important contract for the firm to risk allowing her emotions to take control of her life, and so she had suppressed what she had been feeling, had forced herself to go on, so that now, although she was over the acuteness of realising that Giles had not loved her, although she was fiercely glad that she had discovered the truth about him in time, although she no longer felt the slightest degree of desire *for* him, she was still having to come to terms with the physical and mental effect of the strain she had imposed on her mind and body.

'Stress', her doctor had called it. She knew it was the delayed effect of discovering the truth about Giles. Of having to confront the fact that for her, at least, the term 'having it all' was no more than a cruel joke. Thank God only she knew how willingly she would have given up running the company single-handedly, how willingly she would have shared her responsibilities with Giles. How willingly she would have played a smaller role in the company in order to give herself up to the enjoyment of being a wife and mother. She had been *so* stupid, she acknowledged cynically. Men did not fall in love with women like her. Men found successful career women intimidating, frightening almost, or at least that was what she was beginning to believe.

The coffee Daniel brought her smelled tempting and fragrant. She wrapped her hands around the mug, savouring the rich scent.

'Take it easy,' Daniel warned her, watching her drink it eagerly. 'It isn't decaffeinated, I'm afraid, and your stomach will still be pretty weak.'

'Not when it comes to this,' Angelica assured him with a grin. Piping hot, strong coffee was one of her vices; Tom constantly teased her about the fact that, although she was quite happy to refuse alcohol, despite several attempts she had never quite been able to give up her addiction to her coffee.

'Ah, a fellow addict,' Daniel said now, returning her smile.

When he smiled his whole face changed, she thought breathlessly, as her heart hammered against her ribs in helpless reaction to the shock of her awareness of his sudden and totally unexpected warmth.

'It's disgraceful, isn't it?' she managed to say shakily. 'Nearly all my friends have switched to decaffeinated, and I feel horrendously guilty about not following suit. I've tried a couple of times.'

She was gabbling, frantically trying to fill the silence which had suddenly become very intimate and dangerous. And yet why was she reacting like this simply because a man smiled at her? Was she really so low in self-esteem, so helplessly vulnerable that all it took to overthrow her determined resolution to live her life on her own was one single smile? Did she really crave intimacy with another human being so much that she was pathetically ready to snatch at that smile, to read into it something which common sense told her could not possibly be there? What was wrong with her? She had a good life, a full and satisfying life, good friends like Tom. So why was she constantly aware of this aching emptiness inside her?

'Something wrong?'

The soft question startled her. Her glance flickered nervously to meet his; the cool blue eyes were watching her steadily, assessingly.

She swallowed back her automatic denial, knowing he would see it for the lie it was, and substituted a half-truth instead, shaking her head and saying, 'Not really. I was just wishing I hadn't stopped for that meal.'

'Because it made you ill, or because that illness made you dependent on me?'

His challenge silenced her. She had known instinctively that he would be perceptive, but not how perceptive nor how quick to recognise what she had thought was known only to herself.

'No one likes to feel dependent on a stranger,' she responded guardedly.

She had finished her coffee, and as he leaned across her to remove her mug she flinched back automatically. She was becoming so dangerously aware of him in all the ways she should not be doing that merely being with him was becoming the kind of emotional and physical strain she simply could not handle.

'Is it because I'm a stranger, or because I'm a man?' he asked her bluntly.

She couldn't stop the colour sweeping over her skin, hating the way he made her feel as gauche and awkward as a child.

'You did what had to be done and I'm—I'm grateful to you for it,' she told him uncomfortably.

'You might be grateful to me but you still shy away from me as though you expect me to pounce on you at any moment,' he told her tautly. 'Is that the reason you're so anxious to move next door, even though both of us know damn well that you still aren't strong enough to manage on your own?'

'No,' she denied immediately, horrified by what he was saying. Did he really think her so immature, so stupid that she could possibly imagine he was that kind of man? Far from it . . . The truth was . . .

The truth was that it was *herself* she was afraid of. Her *own* reactions which she feared. Her *own* needs which she dreaded getting out of hand.

He studied her for a moment and then said quietly, 'Good. Well, now that we've got that out of the way, let's not have any more nonsense about you moving next door until you're fully fit, shall we? And while we're on the subject, conscious or unconscious you're in no danger from me. I don't get my kicks from that kind of abuse, no matter how attractive and tempting the woman.'

Angelica stared at him, knowing that her entire body was suffused with a hot colour that he couldn't avoid noticing.

He had described her as attractive, as tempting. Surely he must be exaggerating, flattering her. He couldn't *possibly* mean that he found *her* attractive, and she was a fool if she allowed herself to think so. More than a fool . . . Hadn't she learned anything from her experiences with Giles? Hadn't she told herself over and over again that from now on she would live her life independently, that she would not allow the

kind of emotions rioting through her right now any
place in her life?

Why, when for the last twelve months the thought
of becoming emotionally involved with anyone else
had caused her to feel the most acute fear and tension,
had she suddenly changed like this, overnight almost,
between one breath and the next so that she had arrived at the cottage as one woman and come round
from her illness to discover she had become another?

Was it because subconsciously the intimacy between
them, even though it had been an intimacy of necessity and not desire, had had such an effect on her
that she now found it impossible to look on Daniel
as a stranger? Was *that* why she was so intensely aware
of him? Was *that* why she felt this breathless, aching
need crawling through the pit of her stomach whenever
he came too close to her? Was *that* why she was acting
like a complete fool, and now compounding that folly
by stupidly agreeing that she would continue to stay
with him? What on earth was the matter with her?
She *knew* how imperative it was that she broke this
dangerous intimacy now before she became even more
enmeshed in these stupid feelings. So why *wasn't* she
doing so? Why *wasn't* she moving heaven and earth
to protect herself from the danger he represented? Because she was a fool, that was why, she told herself
bitterly, as Daniel picked up both their mugs and made
them a second cup of coffee.

In the end it was another three days before she was
strong enough for Daniel to agree that she could
manage alone and move into Tom's cottage.

During that time, he had learned far more about her than she had about him. He had a gift for drawing people out, she discovered, a way of encouraging her to talk about herself without making her feel as though he were probing or prying. He made her feel that he was genuinely interested in her, that it was important to him to learn about her.

Only when it came to her relationship with Giles was she deliberately cautious, unwilling to admit to him how much of a fool she had been.

It had been raining all morning. Daniel had disappeared to the farm after breakfast. She had wanted to go with him, but he had said that he thought the walk might be too taxing for her.

Unwilling to press her company on him, when perhaps he was using their need for fresh milk and groceries as an excuse to have some time to himself, she had forborne to point out that they could have driven there, saying coolly instead that it was time she started packing up ready to move next door.

She had been ashamed to discover how much she disliked going back to sleeping in her own night-dresses when Daniel had brought her things out of her car for her; how much she missed the intimacy of wearing his shirts.

Her wayward imagination had even managed to convince her that the scent of him was somehow or other impregnated into the fabric so that when she slept it was almost like sleeping in his arms.

That thought had panicked her so much that she had spent all of the following morning avoiding Daniel. She wasn't used to this intense sensual awareness of a man. Even when she had believed herself in love with Giles, that love had been more cerebral than sensual. Then she had been relieved rather than resentful when he had shown no inclination to make love to her, accepting it when he'd told her that he wanted their physical relationship to be something special and treasured, something precious that would begin with their marriage.

It was only later that she had realised almost inadvertently that he had cold-bloodedly and callously intended that by refusing to make love to her he would send her into such a frenzy of need that she wouldn't look too closely at his reasons for rushing her into marriage. It had never even occurred to him that she was so sexually inexperienced that she had no awareness of the kind of sexual deprivation he'd believed he was inflicting on her.

And yet now, and still with that same lack of actual experience, she was deeply and intensely aware of a need growing within herself, a foolish, almost adolescent urge to behave in a way that was totally out of character for her, an awareness that time was running out; that soon she would be thirty and that because of her dedication to her work there had been no space in her life for her to experience anything else.

But why *this* man? Was it because of their enforced intimacy, because she was completely if temporarily removed from everything and everyone that was familiar to her? An opportunity in fact to behave in a way she would never normally have contemplated? Or was it simply because she knew that in desiring Daniel she was completely safe from indulging in anything more dangerous than silly daydreams? Because she knew that he felt no corresponding desire for her. She tried to imagine how she would feel cooped up alone here with a man who was sexually interested in her, a man who did desire her. She would be horrified of course... Unless—unless that man was Daniel. Ridiculous! Of course she didn't want him to desire her. She had made an irrevocable decision after Giles that she was never going to get involved emotionally with a man again. And she intended to stick with that decision.

So why was she allowing herself to dream these stupidly impossible daydreams about Daniel, a man she had known for less than a week, a man who, despite the fact that he had drawn her into revealing to him a good deal about her own life, had told her nothing of his?

She knew little more about him now than she had done when she first recovered consciousness. His name was Daniel Forbes. He had been living here in the cottage for the past six months. Where he had lived before that she had no idea. Nor did she know how he earned his living, or if indeed he did actually work. When she had tried clumsily to question him about this he had either ignored her or turned the conversation in another direction.

She was beginning to suspect that his limp was the result of some kind of accident, but again he had told her so little about himself and his life that this was only an assumption, and remembering her gullibility over Giles's past had led her to reminding herself that surely only someone with something to conceal would refuse to be open about themselves. She found that entangled with her growing physical awareness of Daniel was a knotted thread of suspicion.

Was she, she wondered, doomed to be attracted only to men who potentially would cause her pain?

And yet there were other times—times when Daniel had made her forget her suspicions, when he had made her laugh with his rueful descriptions of his first attempts at sailing and fishing, times when they had played Scrabble and he had astounded her with the breadth and depth of his knowledge, pointing surely to a man with considerable intelligence.

But that did not necessarily mean that he used that intelligence constructively. He spoke casually about going out with the small local fishing fleet, about working on the farm helping to bring in the crops, but in such a way that she gained the impression that, while he was flexible enough to make himself at home in either world, he was in reality not a permanent part of them, that he was in essence an itinerant.

And of his past he told her almost nothing at all. She knew from an idle comment that he was thirty-five years old and that he was not and never had been married, but she had no idea whether he had any other family.

She, on the other hand, she realised to her own chagrin, had told him so much about herself that he could virtually have written her biography. Only when it came to Giles had she kept silent, partly out of a desire to conceal her own folly, and partly because some deeply rooted feminine instinct made her reluctant to admit to him that she, at close to thirty, was as sexually inexperienced as a girl of eighteen.

She had talked a lot about Tom, about his role in her life, about their friendship and her gratitude to

him, and it was only then that she had seen a deeper
glimpse of the hidden Daniel.

'You're lucky,' he had told her quietly. 'Good
friends are hard to find.'

Later she had wondered if she had been imagining
the aloneness behind the quiet words; if she had foolishly allowed herself to read into them a suggestion
that *he* needed friendship. And if he did, was
friendship really what she wanted from him?

It was certainly safer than this compelling, urgent
need that seemed to grow more intense with every
passing day, rather than less.

She had hoped that living in such close proximity
to him would reveal flaws in his nature which would
quickly ensure that she saw him in a more realistic
light, but so far this had not happened, and tomorrow morning she was moving into Tom's cottage.
She ought to have been glad. After all, privacy was
what she had come down here for, a time alone to
recoup her mental and physical strengths, to recharge
her batteries. The company required her full-time attention and she was all too conscious that of late it
had not been getting it, that she had been relying more
and more often on her second-in-command.

Not that Paul seemed to mind. He was young and
ambitious and he seemed to thrive on the challenge—
just as she had once done? Was it purely because of
Giles that she no longer enjoyed that challenge, that
the responsibility for the company had become almost
an onerous burden? That she felt almost as though
running it was depriving her of the right to live her
own life, to find fulfilment of a different kind?

The weather had been blustery and wet, but before leaving for the farm Daniel had told her that the forecast was promising warmer, brighter spells.

'If it's fine tomorrow, we could start you off with a gentle stroll ... See how you feel after that. It's surprising how long it can take to get over something like this.'

She had wanted to ask how he knew, but had refrained, knowing her question wouldn't be answered.

Their relationship, if you could call it that, was decidedly one-sided, she reflected frustratedly now. Sometimes she felt like a child under the control of an adult—that she was vulnerable to Daniel in a way that he could never be vulnerable to her. And yet tomorrow, when she had moved into Tom's cottage, there would be nothing to compel her to continue with their acquaintanceship. She could if she wished simply thank him for everything he had done and then quietly and firmly close her door on him. And yet she knew already that she wouldn't do so, that she would give in to the dictates of her foolish and unwary heart.

He was gone far longer than she had anticipated. She actually found that she had started to pace the kitchen anxiously, glancing towards the window, her determination to occupy herself preparing for her move next door forgotten.

This was ridiculous, she told herself, sitting down and trying to concentrate on the book she had picked up randomly from the packed bookshelves in the small sitting-room. She wondered how many, if any, of the books were Daniel's. They showed a wide-ranging span of interests, and included some of her own favourite works of fiction as well as technical and

scientific manuals, and biographies on many leading
historical and political people.

The book, a relatively new one by one of her
favourite authors, failed to hold her attention.
Normally when Daniel went to the farm he was back
within the hour, an hour and a half at the most. This
time he had been gone for over two hours. Supposing
something had happened to him? With his limp...

She was being ridiculous, she told herself, and
added to her anxiety was a self-defensive anger that
she could actually allow herself to be so concerned
over a man who was virtually a stranger.

It was almost as though in some subtle and
dangerous way he had become important to her, that
she had actually almost become dependent on him,
and that terrified her, making her tense and shiver,
as she refused to give in to the impulse to snap her
book closed and rush outside to look for him.

What was the matter with her? She who had learned
the hard way how necessary it was to be self-sufficient,
first through her father's death and then the subsequent realisation that from now on she was going
to have to find a way of supporting her mother both
emotionally and financially, and of keeping the
company going, and then later with Giles.

She hadn't realised until recently, until her illness
had forced on her time to think, how much she had
come to dread the heavy weight of her own responsibilities, and how much a part of her longed to
escape from them.

But now she had something far more dangerous and
invasive to worry about.

How *could* she have become so dependent on Daniel in such a short space of time? *Was* it because of her illness, of her helplessness, then? Or was it because of something deeper, something more worrying?

Half an hour later, when he had still not returned, it took every ounce of will-power she possessed to stop herself from setting off down the track that led to the farm to look for him.

She told herself that there were any number of reasons why he could have been delayed, that if he chose to disappear without any explanation it was his affair and not hers.

And yet when eventually she heard him opening the back door, the feelings that engulfed her were so intense that she could actually feel tears of anger and relief burning her eyes.

As she blinked them away she heard him saying easily, 'Sorry I was so long, but it occurred to me that since this is our last evening together we ought to mark the occasion in some special way, and so I walked down to the village to buy a bottle of wine to go with the beef Mrs Davies sold me.'

He was smiling at her, casually removing his jacket so that she was momentarily distracted by the subtle movement of taut male muscles, her emotions on a dangerous roller-coaster of instability that held her caught between rage and remorse as she listened to his explanation for his absence.

'What's wrong?' he asked her perceptively, putting his purchases down on the work-top and frowning as he came towards her.

As first she tried to lie, shaking her head in denial of his question, but when he caught hold of her

shoulders and shook her in gentle reproof her con-
straint gave way and she found herself telling him
shakily that she had been worried about him—
concerned.

'Because of this, you mean?' he questioned her, releasing her and briefly touching his leg.

She flushed uncomfortably, recognising that she had
no right to feel concern, and that, moreover, he like
most men would probably not welcome her emotional
reaction, but, instead of appearing annoyed or irritated, he simply looked at her for a long time, a slow,
searching look that made her muscles tense and her
heart start to beat increasingly fast.

'I was thoughtless,' he said at last. 'I should have
realised you'd be concerned. It's been a long time since
anyone worried about my welfare.'

It was a strange moment. A tense silence enveloped
them both. Angelica discovered that she was holding
her breath as though in anticipation. But anticipation
of what? Why did she suddenly feel it was imperative
for her to rush into husky, too fast speech as she
almost gabbled, 'Never mind. The thought of eating
that steak more than makes up for it.'

And she turned away from him, picking up the milk
and eggs, saying with false brightness, 'I'll put these
in the fridge, shall I?'

'Not all of them,' Daniel cautioned her. 'Half of
it's for you—for tomorrow—but you might as well
put them in this fridge here for now.'

The reminder that tomorrow she would be on her
own brought home to her how unwise it was of her
to allow herself to become so involved with him, and
made her question *why* she was doing it. He had cer-

tainly not encouraged or invited her to do so. No—her folly was her own responsibility, and so was anything she might suffer because of it.

But she wasn't *going* to suffer... Not this time. She had learned her lesson with Giles, hadn't she? Hadn't she?

CHAPTER FOUR

As ANGELICA had already discovered, Daniel was a proficient cook, and indeed proficient in every way domestically, but without any of the self-conscious flourishing of his talents she had often found so irritating in some of her married friends, whose husbands seemed to make a tremendous issue of their domestic talents, adopting a boring air of self-righteousness, or even worse becoming more expert and vocal on such matters than their partners. Angelica fully believed in a mutual sharing of domestic chores, especially when both partners in a relationship had careers, but hadn't been able to help wondering if the assistance received was sometimes worth the enormous amount of ego-stroking and lavish praise the female halves of such partnerships had to lavish upon the male in return for it.

When Daniel expressed concern over the wisdom of her eating steak when she was so newly recovered from her food poisoning, she assured him firmly that in normal circumstances she possessed an extremely sturdy digestive system.

Her vehemence made him laugh, and after her initial surprise—laughter was something she wasn't used to sharing with other people, not even with her closest friends—she too laughed at her own determination.

'You're obviously an only child,' Daniel commented as he started to prepare their meal.

'Yes, I am,' she agreed. 'But how did you know?'

'Simple—you aren't used to being teased. Most only children aren't. I wasn't myself until I went away to school.' He must have seen the pity in her face, because he added calmly, 'It wasn't that bad, and my father didn't really have any option. My mother was killed in a car accident when I was eight, and, given the choice between employing someone to take care of me full-time, and perhaps isolating me from contact with other children, or sending me away to school, he opted for a boarding-school.

'I thought we'd just have a salad with the steak, and I managed to get Mrs Davies to part with some of her precious wild strawberries for afters.'

'I'll do the salad, shall I?' Angelica offered.

'Mm. If you wouldn't mind.'

It surprised Angelica how companionably they could work together; she wasn't used to this kind of domestic intimacy. Her father had been a rather reserved, withdrawn man, old-fashioned in his outlook, firmly believing that man was the provider and woman the homemaker and that the two spheres should not overlap.

Consequently, as a child she had seen very little of him, and had grown up knowing very little about the male sex, which was probably why she had been such a fool where Giles was concerned.

A more aware, more knowledgeable woman would never have fallen so easily for his facile charm. It galled her now that she could ever have been so stupid.

The rich smell of the sauce Daniel was preparing made her mouth water. Her stomach felt hollow and empty after her illness. She was very, very hungry, she realised, as she busied herself with her salad.

'I hope you don't mind eating in here,' Daniel asked her when the steaks were nearly ready. 'The cottage doesn't boast a separate dining-room, and since I don't normally do much entertaining . . .'

'In here's fine,' Angelica assured him. 'I like this room.'

She was telling him the truth. There was something warm and comfortable about the kitchen with its shabby furniture and its warm Aga; she felt at home here, relaxed and at ease. Which was very strange given the fact that she had not grown up in these kind of surroundings, and so had no nostalgia for them; neither was she used to the kind of domestic intimacy she was now sharing with Daniel, and yet she felt completely relaxed with him, reluctant to accept that this would be their last evening together, reluctant for this odd and totally unexpected interlude to end. As always, the moment these traitorous emotions hit her she panicked, whipping herself up into a state of mental alert and tension, forcing herself to deny what she was feeling, telling herself that she would be glad when she was safely alone in Tom's cottage, that in fact she would find it infinitely preferable if there had never been a cottage next door to Tom's, if there had never been a Daniel.

'Steak's ready,' Daniel told her, breaking into her panic-stricken thoughts.

She discovered as she sat down that she was trembling slightly, a physical reaction to her emotional turmoil, and a sharp reminder that, despite the fact that she felt she was fully recovered, her bout of food poisoning had left her physically weakened. Daniel had warned her that it could be months before her body fully returned to normal after such a very bad attack. She had responded testily that she was as strong as a horse and that she was already fully recovered, but now, feeling the spasms of weakness seizing her muscles, knowing that the faint beads of perspiration dampening her skin weren't caused only by her panic over her dangerous emotions, she found herself mentally admitting that she was still not one hundred per cent recovered.

She *was* hungry though, and the steak had a flavour like none she had ever known. The wine Daniel had bought to go with their meal was smooth and mellow, and gradually, as they ate and talked, she discovered that she was telling him far more about herself than she had ever told anyone.

Several times she told herself she must put a guard on her unruly tongue, blaming the richness of the wine and the fact that she so rarely drank for her unusual openness.

It was only when Daniel remarked casually, 'I know you're not married, but have you——?' that she became aware of danger and interrupted him quickly, saying,

'I haven't pried into your private life, Daniel, so——'

'I'm not prying,' he retaliated just as quickly. 'I was simply wondering if there was a man in your life who might object to the fact that I find you a highly desirable woman.'

The total unexpectedness of it took her breath away. She had just raised her glass to her lips, and now she took a quick gulp of wine and then almost choked on it as her whole nervous system went into frantic overdrive.

She blinked and focused uncertainly on Daniel's face, wondering dizzily if she was imagining things. He looked so calm and normal sitting there eating his steak. He looked as he had looked the whole time she had been staying here: pleasant and slightly remote, not at all like a man who had just said what she thought she had heard him say.

'What's wrong?' Daniel asked her, suddenly curt and slightly forbidding. 'Is the fact that I find you attractive so offensive to you that——?'

'No—no—it isn't that,' Angelica managed to stammer.

'And there isn't anyone special in your life,' he pursued.

'Not now,' Angelica admitted flatly, and then cursed herself as she saw him frown.

'You've been married. You're divorced,' he guessed.

Angelica shook her head, unable to lie. 'No—no, I was engaged—well, almost. I'd made a commitment to—to someone. I thought he'd made the same commitment to me.'

To her horror she found her throat was clogged with tears. Why, when she knew what a fortunate escape she had had? Why cry now when she hadn't allowed herself to cry before? What was there after all to cry for apart from her own folly?

'He left you?'

'Not exactly.' Briefly she explained what had happened, stopping breathlessly halfway through her explanation to take another quick gulp of her wine and to marvel a little hazily at what she was doing.

Not even to her closest friends had she confided as much as she was now confiding to Daniel. What was it about him that made her feel she could trust him? That made her *want* to confide in him, that made her feel so secure, so safe, so protected almost?

She watched now as he refilled her wine glass, protesting uncertainly, 'I shouldn't really. It's going straight to my head.'

But nevertheless, more out of nervousness than anything else, she picked up the glass and started toying with it, before taking a small sip and then another.

'Do you still love him?' Daniel asked her quietly.

'No. But I still feel—I don't know—sort of raw inside for being such a fool. A woman of my age... I ought to have realised.'

'What? That he was lying to you? That he was using you? Age isn't any protection against that kind of vulnerability.'

'No, perhaps not, but I ought to have realised when he didn't want to——'

She bit her lip, angry with herself for her own stupidity. Another few seconds and she would have been telling Daniel that Giles had never made love to her. That final humiliation was something she hadn't been able to bring herself to tell anyone. It had left a deep wound that still hadn't healed, that realisation that, not only had Giles not loved her, but that he hadn't desired her either, that he had found her so lacking as a woman that sexually he had been totally uninterested in her. It didn't matter that she herself had been lacking in any deep sexual curiosity about him. She had put that down to the fact that her sheltered upbringing and general ignorance about men had made her sexually naïve and immature. Giles had been neither of those things though, as she had brutally discovered when she had found him with someone else, and now, although she might not regret the loss of the man, she still ached inside with the knowledge that she had been rejected as a woman.

'When he didn't want to what?' Daniel pounced. His wine glass was just over half full; the bottle was nearly empty, which meant that he must have drunk exactly as much as she, and yet it didn't seem to be having anything like the same effect on him as it was having on her.

'When he didn't what, Angelica?' he pressed.

Her throat had gone very dry. She wanted badly to lie to him and casually pass off her slip-up by saying something like, 'Oh, when he didn't want to introduce me to his friends, that's all,' but she knew she simply could not do it with anything like conviction.

She touched her tongue-tip to her lips in a nervously betraying gesture, licking their dryness while she hunted frantically for something to say, wondering how on earth she had ever got herself into this mess.

What was wrong with her? she asked herself bitterly. Was she so desperate for male appreciation and attention that the moment a man flirted casually with her and commented that he found her attractive, she instantly had to regale him with her entire life-story?

'What didn't he do?' she heard Daniel insist, and suddenly her pride gave way beneath much stronger needs. Recklessly ignoring the panic-stricken voice of warning inside her brain, she told him with husky defiance,

'When he didn't want to—to make love to me. I should have realised *then,* but, like a fool, I thought...' She shook her head helplessly. 'Go on, laugh if you want to. I expect I would in your shoes.'

'Believe me, the last thing I feel like doing is laughing,' Daniel assured her grimly. So grimly that she forgot her self-conscious anguish and stared at him, trying to read what lay behind the hard darkness of his eyes, wondering what it was that she had said to provoke the bitter anger flaring in them.

'Unfortunately there *are* human beings like that, who enjoy wounding and maiming, who take pleasure in inflicting the kind of pain that does not kill, but which instead festers, leaving a poison that spreads over the whole of their victim's life. You must be very strong emotionally to have survived that kind of treachery.'

Was that really how he saw her—as someone strong? She thought of all the nights she had lain awake tormented by self-doubt and anguish, of all the pain and self-analysis she had gone through, of the aloneness she now endured, of the stress which had finally resulted in her coming here.

'Strength isn't a virtue men look for in a woman,' she told him bitterly.

'Oh, yes, it is,' he contradicted. 'It's just that most of us don't choose to admit it. A weak, clinging woman might appeal to an immature, insecure man, who needs that kind of dependence on him, but he soon grows tired of it and of the woman, poor creature. A woman with her own special strengths and inner resources is something else again.'

He said it so softly that it was several seconds before she realised how intensely he meant what he was saying. His eyes were shadowed as though he were looking not at her, but back into the past, and she wondered what on earth lay there to make him look like that, to make him feel like that, and then just as she was about to ask him, to question him as he had questioned her, he stunned her by asking directly, 'Have you *ever* had a lover, Angelica?'

She was too stunned to lie, her eyes widening as she absorbed the question, recognised its intimacy, felt her body as well as her emotions react to it, and responded automatically without thinking.

'No. No, I haven't. Does it show so much?'

'No. No, it doesn't show at all. If you hadn't told me tonight about Giles, if I'd gone on my first impression of you when you arrived here, I'd have put you down as a sophisticated and experienced woman; not a woman who cares to indulge in casual sex—you obviously value yourself far too highly for that—but a woman none the less who knows what it is to share passion and desire.'

'I'm afraid the truth must be rather disappointing,' she responded huskily, bending her head over her wine glass so that her hair swung forward and hid her expression from him. She felt such a fool. Why on earth had she told him so much?

The unexpected touch of his fingers against her skin as he brushed her hair away forced her to look up directly into his eyes. They were glittering with an unexpected heat that made her stomach muscles clench and her body tense.

'Who said I was disappointed?' he asked her softly.

She had made the remark instinctively, defensively, not expecting him to take her up on it, to challenge her so directly and thus imbue their conversation with a far more personal intimacy than she had intended it to have.

From somewhere she found the courage to add recklessly, 'And please don't tell me that you're the kind of man who finds the idea of a woman of twenty-eight still being a virgin—a—challenge or in some way exciting, because I won't believe you.'

'Good, because I'm not,' he replied promptly. 'But I find *you* exciting, Angelica.'

It stopped the breath in her throat, froze all her responses, made her focus on his face and stare into his eyes, the expression in her own unguarded and naked for the whole of half a dozen heavy heartbeats, while she assimilated his quiet words and in a panic tried to deny them.

He *couldn't* find her exciting. She *wasn't* exciting. She was a twenty-eight-year-old virgin, whom no man had *ever* found exciting.

Out of her panic, she recognised later that she said the very worst possible thing she could have said, challenging him almost, although that was not what she intended when she delivered her flat, emotionless denial of what he had just said.

'I don't believe you.'

'Why not?'

She tried to think of a reason and found that her mind had gone dismayingly blank, and in the end all she could manage was a feeble, 'Well, men just *don't* find me exciting.'

'Because they don't *tell* you so.' He sounded amused now, and suddenly she felt angry both with him and with herself. She stood up, pushing herself away from the table and then finding that she had to cling to it as dizziness hit her.

'I'm not a complete idiot,' she told him bitterly. 'I am aware of how the male sex behaves when it experiences desire. Oh, not personally, maybe, but I'm a great observer of life; people like me always are— we don't have much alternative. I *have* seen how a man reacts when he meets a woman he finds attractive.'

'Really.'

Daniel too was standing up and for one breathless moment she actually thought he was going to come round to her side of the table, and take hold of her and . . .

The disappointment that welled through her when he didn't, but walked past her instead, made her bite her lip and burn with a fierce inner resentment both of him and of herself. What was it about her that made her so vulnerable, so stupid? Had she really thought that he meant it, that he wanted her? Hadn't she already learned her lesson? He was just playing a game with her, just whiling away their final hours together, just amusing himself at her expense.

He was doing something by the sink. She heard him turn on the tap but refused to look round. She didn't want to look at him, she recognised, because she was frightened that if she did so that uncomfortable aching, yearning sensation in the pit of her stomach would fill her again, rendering her helpless to fight against the slow pulse of need he seemed to arouse so effortlessly inside her.

'You've got to taste Mrs Davies's strawberries,' she heard him saying. 'I almost forgot about them. You aren't allergic to them, I hope.'

She wanted to fib and say that she was, to react childishly and petulantly and storm off up to her room in a fit of sulks, but thankfully she managed to subdue the impulse and assure him as casually as though they had been discussing nothing more intimate than the weather that she was longing to taste the farmer's wife's soft fruit.

She still couldn't look at him though, rigidly keeping her back to him, but all the time intensely conscious of every small movement of his body. And yet for all that her ears were straining to catch every movement he made, he still managed to leave the sink and walk up behind her without her being in the least bit aware of it until she heard him saying, 'Here are your strawberries.'

The shock of knowing that he was standing directly behind her made her turn her head far too quickly so that she immediately became dizzy and disorientated. She tried to stand up, without knowing why other than that she had to escape from him, and yet in standing up she had effectively moved even closer to him.

Mercifully he seemed to have mistaken the cause of her reaction, because as he took hold of her upper arms she heard him saying urgently, 'Angelica, are you all right? Are you feeling ill?' And then, when she didn't make an immediate reply, he swept her up off her feet and carried her over to the chair beside the Aga, muttering under his breath, 'I *knew* you shouldn't have had that damn steak.'

'It *wasn't* the steak,' she protested automatically, the words muffled against his chest as he paused in the act of releasing her to stare frowningly into her eyes. 'Really, I'm fine.'

'So fine that you looked as though you were about to pass out,' he told her grittily, demanding, 'If it wasn't the steak, then what the hell was it?'

She could have fibbed, ought to have done and in fact fully intended to do so, manufacturing some excuse about the wine and her own lack of tolerance for it, and it was certainly true that the alcohol did seem to have loosened all her normal inhibitions, did seem to have removed from her behaviour the constraints she normally imposed on it, did seem to have made her feel extraordinarily and dangerously incautious. But it wasn't the wine that made her take that fateful and betraying step of letting her glance slide from his eyes to his mouth and linger there while her tongue-tip unconsciously stroked her own mouth, relieving its sudden dryness.

'Angelica.'

Panic suddenly seized her with the realisation of what she was inviting. As his head bent towards her,

his hands suddenly tightening on her arms, she
trembled openly and moaned a frantically protesting
'no', which both of them knew was not the denial it
seemed.

Certainly there was nothing rejecting or reluctant
about the way her lips clung to the slow caress of his,
her panic subsiding, forgotten in the slow, sweet wash
of pleasure that seized her.

It was such a gentle kiss, such an exploratory, tender
pressure of mouth against mouth, as though he was
deliberately giving her the opportunity to draw back,
as though he had sensed her panic and understood
how much she needed this restrained tenderness to ease
it from her and reassure her. As though he was deliberately giving her the time to become accustomed
to this intimacy with him, and her own reaction to
his unfamiliar maleness.

His body imprisoned hers within the soft depths of
the chair, but it wasn't a threatening imprisonment,
just as the pressure of his kiss wasn't being brutally
enforced on her, just as the grip of his hands on her
arms was such that she knew instinctively she only
had to move, to protest, and she would immediately
be set free; the smallest signal that this wasn't what
she wanted and it would be over. She knew that as
well as she knew her own name, just as well as she
knew that in allowing this kiss to continue she was
inviting the kind of intimacy, the kind of vulnerability that could only lead to further pain. So why
didn't she stop him?

Her senses knew the answer. Dizzily, greedily almost
they drank in the pleasure he was giving them, intoxicated by his scent, his taste, his weight against her

body, his touch against her skin, the heat he was generating between them.

Why, when she had thought she loved Giles so deeply, had she never once with him been aware of him as a man in the way that she was now so overwhelmingly and sharply aware of Daniel's maleness? *Why* had she never hungered for everything that was male in Giles with the same fierce, elemental hunger she could now feel for Daniel?

She was hungry for him in a way that both excited and alarmed her. The tender, exploratory pressure of his mouth was no longer enough. She wanted to bite at it, to tease it with her tongue, to feel its hungry pressure. She wanted . . . She gave a deep shudder and made a small anguished sound deep in her throat as she recognised how disturbingly quickly she had gone from apprehension to arousal. And it was no use pretending she wasn't aroused. At least not to herself.

What did amaze her was how easily and quickly she, who had never really experienced this kind of sexual intensity before, could recognise so immediately what it was that was happening to her.

She didn't need any experience to tell her that the tight ache in her breasts was caused by her need to feel Daniel's hands against her skin, or that the fierce pulse beating urgently lower down in her body was caused by its feminine need to feel the maleness of him stroking deep within her wanton flesh.

Shocked as she was to discover that she could be aroused so quickly and so intensely, she was honest enough to admit to herself that it wasn't simply the fact that Daniel was kissing her that was responsible for her immediate reaction to him. Her own thoughts, her own awareness of him as a man, her own awareness of the effect he had on her had already primed her body to be receptive to his touch. And not merely receptive, she acknowledged weakly as she tried to fight for some self-control.

She wanted him with a need which she had always felt belonged to women of a far different calibre from herself. She wanted him as hungrily and immediately as though she were a woman with a succession of lovers behind her and a very experienced awareness of her own needs and appetites.

When she had contemplated making love with Giles, it had been with a certain amount of hesitancy and apprehension, a relief almost that their physical union was something she didn't have to confront until they were married, but now, with Daniel, there was no hesitancy, no apprehension and certainly no reluctance.

He was still kissing her, feathering small delicate kisses along her jaw, exploring the delicate whorls of her ear, making her moan and sending her into an agony of need as she clung helplessly to his arms, biting her bottom lip as she fought to suppress the betraying moans clogging her throat. And yet when his mouth did return to hers, as though the hand that caressed the taut flesh of her throat had registered her ruthlessly silenced 'please', instead of behaving with dignified restraint, instead of passively allowing *him* to kiss *her*, she gave in to her earlier need and bit frantically at his bottom lip, digging her nails into the hard muscles of his back as she lost her battle to control the effect he was having on her.

That her behaviour was so totally out of character, that even to contemplate it in the privacy of her own thoughts would normally have been enough to shock her with self-disgust and disbelief that she could ever, ever act in such a way, was something that never even managed to surface past the fierce ache of need that engulfed her, and Daniel, far from appearing to find it shocking, responded to her fevered urgency with such satisfying immediacy and recognition, pressing her deep into the depth of the chair, his hands tangling in her hair, hard and warm against her scalp as he held her a willing prisoner beneath the fierce ravishment of his mouth, that she quite unconsciously made delirious sounds of pleasure that he told her huskily reminded him of a cat starting to purr. For some reason his words made her shiver erotically and arch her body as though she wanted to rub it against him as enticingly as that same animal wanting to be stroked.

Never when she had contemplated the act of making love had she envisaged that it could be accompanied by words, promises, pleas, indistinct sometimes and yet so intensely arousing that to hear them, to recognise the arousal and desire they cloaked, was almost as erotic as the touch of his hands and mouth. And if she had never contemplated a man saying these things to her, even less had she imagined herself saying similar things, to make—making desperate pleas... giving soft whispers of lavish praise, allowing herself to be carried away on a tide so deep and full that when Daniel stopped kissing her briefly and then watched her gravely, while his hands unfastened the first button of her blouse, she had no thought of stopping him, no awareness of self-consciousness or

shyness, only a dizzying eagerness to be rid of the
constriction of her clothes, which made her move
restlessly and plaintively beneath his hands, so that
they trembled slightly and she caught the betraying
rasp of his indrawn breath as her urgency seemed to
communicate itself to him, and he wrenched almost
awkwardly at one of the buttons, causing her heart
to pound, not with fear, but with fierce excitement
and pleasure at the thought that he wanted her as
much as she did him.

Why had she never known there would be such a
powerful, glorious sense of freedom in giving full rein
to her own desires? Why had she never realised how
euphoric the knowledge of her own passion could be?

'Angelica...Angel... That's how you feel; too
perfect to be real.' She tasted the husky compliments
on Daniel's lips as his hands cupped her naked breasts,
the rough heat of his palms against her nipples turning
them stiff with excitement and anticipation.

'Touch me, Angelica. Touch me, please. I want to
feel your hands on my body.'

Eagerly she followed his whispered pleas, tugging
impatiently at buttons and fastenings in her need to
explore the male heat of his flesh. She felt him tremble
violently as her fingertips skimmed the hot satin
hardness of his chest, urging away his shirt.

She kissed his throat, lost in a delirious voyage of
discovery, culminating in a sudden surge of feminine
excitement that stopped abruptly when she flicked her
tongue delicately against the button hardness of his
nipple. Unable to resist the lure of her own instincts,
she covered the small area of flesh with her mouth,

teasing it gently with her teeth and then not so gently as she felt the heat pulse through her own body.

Lost in her own growing pleasure, she felt an abrupt shock when Daniel suddenly took hold of her, wrenching her away from his body, his voice rough and raw with warning as he demanded, 'Have you *any* idea what you're doing to me? How fast you're pushing me to the edge of my self-control?'

Confusion and uncertainty clouded her eyes. Had she done something wrong, offended him in some way? She was suddenly acutely aware of her lack of experience, of the fact that, while she had undoubtedly enjoyed caressing him, he might not have found her caresses equally welcome.

Embarrassed and guilty, she withdrew from him, saying stiffly, 'I'm sorry. I didn't think. I shouldn't——'

She didn't get any further. Daniel made a taut explosive sound in his throat which visibly tensed the muscles there and demanded, 'You shouldn't have *what*? Made me feel like *this*?'

Before she could stop him, his hand cupped her breast, his lips feathering its quivering tip in much the same way as she had caressed him, but Angelica was beyond recognising that fact, incapable of recognising anything other than the intense surge of pleasure that jolted through her, turning her boneless, turning her stomach into a hollow of liquid excitement and making her moan his name out aloud and cling with desperate hands to his arms. The gentle pressure of his mouth became harder, more urgent, more compelling. She was shivering with emotion and arousal, only half listening to him while Daniel whispered rawly against her flesh that now she knew exactly how she had made him feel.

She heard him but didn't believe him. Couldn't believe that her inexperienced touch could possibly have aroused him to the frenzy of need his had evoked from her. She was still trembling when his mouth slowly released her swollen flesh, still too caught up in the urgency of her feelings to even think of protesting when his mouth burned a path down over the taut flesh of her ribcage and came to rest on the soft swell of her belly, nibbling at the satin softness of her skin as though the taste of it intoxicated him.

'I want you, Angelica,' he told her huskily. 'Right now there's nothing I want more than to take you to bed and make love to you, but I can't . . .'

Her mind registered the words like a blow, stunned by the unexpected force of it, too crippled to retaliate, while her body screamed in silent agony at his cruelty. To have aroused her so intensely, to have allowed her to believe . . . to expect . . . to want . . .

She made a stifled sound of anguish in her throat and tried to pull away from him, but he wouldn't let her go.

'No. Wait. Don't you understand? I *can't* make love to you because I *can't* protect you from the consequences of that lovemaking. I can't protect you from conceiving my child.'

As his words sank in, she knew she ought to be grateful to him, not resentful. She knew one day maybe she would be, but right now . . . Right now she felt humiliated and rejected, raw inside with an ache like one from an open wound. She was intensely conscious of how hard she was finding it to get her aroused body back under control, of how much it ached even now for Daniel's touch, for Daniel's possession.

'I never intended things to go so far,' she heard him telling her, but instead of soothing her, his words only inflamed her anguish. She was the one to blame for what had happened. Not him. She was the one who had deliberately tried to force the pace, who had eagerly and wantonly let her body tell him how much it wanted him.

She felt sick with bitter reaction, nauseously self-contemptuous in a way that not even Giles had made her feel. This was different. Then she had been contemptuous of her emotional folly, this—this physical . . . loss, this wanton desire for a man who plainly did not want her . . . She started to tremble violently, moaning a sharp protest when instead of releasing her so that she could escape to her own room, to privacy and darkness, Daniel continued to hold on to her, pulling her firmly into his arms, imprisoning her against the warm length of his body so that she was almost lying on top of him and intimately conscious of the heat and strength of him.

Her bitter protest was smothered against his skin as he closed his arms around her, one hand soothingly stroking her back, the other refusing to release her, his voice a soft, gentle whisper as he coaxed her to relax. Relax, that was the last thing she wanted to do, and yet oddly, beneath the soothing pressure of his stroking hand, and the soft, mesmeric lull of his voice, she discovered that that was exactly what she *was* doing, all the angry tension and the overwrought desire eased from her body as he gently brought it down from the frenzied heights of arousal to a more restful plain.

Gradually her breathing slowed and deepened, her eyes closing, her body relaxing into sleep.

Glancing wryly into her sleeping face, Daniel wished he could ease the tormenting ache from his own flesh as thoroughly as he had soothed it from hers. He felt guilty that he had allowed things to get so out of hand, but he had never imagined that she would touch him so intimately nor so arousingly. And once she had . . . Well, once she had, the pleasure of feeling her mouth moving against his skin had been far too intense for him to stop her.

As he eased her gently away from him, his body pulsed its aching message of need to stay close to her. It was just as well she had fallen asleep, otherwise . . . otherwise . . . Otherwise he would have been dangerously tempted to go on making love to her and to hell with the consequences.

He was a rational, analytical man who rarely acted on impulse, but now he reflected grimly that there were some needs and impulses over which the brain had precious little control, and unless he wanted them to take over his life completely he had better take Angelica upstairs and leave her safely alone in her own bed.

It was just as well she was moving next door in the morning. Then he would no longer be in the invidious position of having to keep some distance between them, of having not to seem to take advantage of their situation. Then he would be able to establish a proper relationship with her. Smiling softly at her, he bent his head and pressed a lingering kiss on her mouth. In her sleep she mumbled his name and her lips clung moistly to his. He felt his heart start to thunder and his body tense, and, sighing a little, he released her.

CHAPTER FIVE

ANGELICA lay tensely in bed, straining to catch some sound of activity from downstairs. She had woken up half an hour ago, and immediately the events of the previous evening had come flooding back to her. The mere fact that she had been tucked beneath the quilt still half dressed told its own story, and she reflected bitterly that it had no doubt come as a great relief to Daniel when she had so conveniently fallen asleep before things had got too embarrassingly out of hand.

Poor man, all he had probably intended to do was to exchange a few meaningless kisses with her. A pleasant finale to their evening together, their *last* evening together, and she had had to go and make a complete fool of herself by behaving in a way that had been so pathetically over the top that her whole body burned with hot embarrassment even to think of it.

Thank goodness she had already made the decision to take up residence next door. Daniel must be feeling as relieved about that as she was herself. There was really no excuse for the way she had behaved last night, like—like a woman starved of physical affection for so long that her hunger for it had totally overwhelmed her.

She moved uncomfortably in her bed. What had happened to her must have been some sort of physical backlash to Giles's rejection of her. That and the overheated atmosphere of intimacy forced on her by her illness was what had led to her astoundingly stupid behaviour.

The wine hadn't helped, of course. Alcohol was notorious for relaxing one's inhibitions. But surely the desire had to be there in the first place. And that didn't account for the fact that she had felt such an extraordinary intensity of desire for Daniel, only that she had given way to it. And if she was honest with herself, hadn't she really been aware of him as a man for far longer than a mere evening?

Her mind balked at accepting the truth. What kind of woman was she anyway? She who had always felt so safe and so aloof from the vagaries of sexual desire, she who had always assumed that it was a need from which she was never going to suffer. Was it something to do with her age—a woman—something to do with the fact that she was a woman nearing thirty who had suddenly woken up and realised that she was not fulfilling her primary biological function? But it hadn't been a desire to conceive a *child* that had sent her wild in Daniel's arms, had it? It had been *her* need, *her* intense physical ache to make *herself* a part of him. It had been for *her*!

Maybe then it was caused by the stress she had suffered; maybe it was some kind of delayed reaction to losing Giles. Maybe she had even somehow or other transferred on to Daniel the physical desire she should have felt, but never had felt, for Giles.

She pressed her hands to her temples, helplessly wishing she could just close her eyes and make last night disappear from her memory and from Daniel's.

She could hear him moving about downstairs, and, reluctant as she was to face him, the thought of him coming to find her, walking into her bedroom, seeing her lying beneath the quilt where he had placed her and undoubtedly then remembering how she had behaved last night was enough to have her scooting up out of bed and hurrying to get showered and downstairs.

Once she *was* dressed, she lingered as long as she could over packing away her possessions and her clothes, while acknowledging that she could hardly stay upstairs all day.

Taking a deep breath, she opened her bedroom door. The sooner she went down and faced Daniel, the sooner she would be able to escape next door.

Even if he was compassionate enough not to mention last night, it was going to lie between the two of them, creating deep embarrassment on her part and no doubt making him regret that he had ever given in to whatever impulse had moved him to kiss her in the first place.

It was all very well remembering that he had said he wanted her, that he had touched her with passion and need. It was different for men. They were allowed to be carried away by the needs of their flesh. Women were expected to be more circumspect, and anyway, the way she remembered it, *she* was the one whose self-control had snapped so disastrously.

If she had expected Daniel to glibly and sophisticatedly ignore the fact that last night had ever happened, if she had expected him to behave as though it was a subject best not referred to, the moment she stepped into the kitchen she realised her mistake.

He must have heard her coming downstairs because he was waiting for her, watching her with grave scrutiny as she walked into the room.

He came towards her, still studying her, his quiet, 'Are you OK?' making her nerve-endings tingle warningly as she stepped sideways to avoid the hand he held out to her and chose to pretend that she thought he was referring to her original food poisoning by averting her head and saying briefly,

'Yes, I'm fine. In fact, totally recovered. I shan't eat at an unfamiliar restaurant again in a hurry though.'

Out of the corner of her eye, she saw his mouth compress as though he was annoyed. But what had he expected her to say? she wondered nervily as her heart skipped a beat and her pulses started to race.

That she still ached inside for him, that she was confused and afraid of the power of her own desires, that she felt humiliated and ashamed of the way she had behaved, that her mind was full of searing mental images of how she had touched him, her brain ringing with the bitter-sweet betrayal of the pleas she had made to him. Did he really expect her to admit to all of that? Couldn't he *see* how difficult she was finding it just to try to behave normally, when all she really wanted to do was to crawl away and hide herself somewhere until she could come to terms with what was happening to her?

And what *was* happening to her? She knew that physically he affected her in ways that once would have made her laugh in self-derision. She knew that the mere sight of him sent her heartbeat and pulse-rate into such a frenzied burst of over-activity that she

felt she was in danger of hyperventilating. She knew
that this strange aching pain growing inside her like
a grey cloud of melancholy meant that it wasn't just
physically that he affected her, but she also knew that
it would be self-destructive in the extreme to allow
herself to dwell too deeply on any of these things.

From behind her she heard Daniel saying grimly,
'I wasn't referring to your food poisoning and you
know it. Last night we came damn close to being
lovers. When I put you to bed I——'

It was too much. She couldn't bear any more. For
a man whom she had believed to be extraordinarily
sensitive and aware for one of his sex, he was suddenly displaying such a cruel disregard of her feelings
that she could only believe that he must actually be
enjoying inflicting this humiliation on her.

She had tried ignoring the issue, pretending that it
hadn't happened ... He hadn't taken the hint, hadn't
seemed to accept that it was something she just could
not bear to discuss, but he couldn't force her to respond to him.

Compressing her lips, she hurried over to the coffee-
machine and picked up the jug of hot coffee, pouring
some into a mug. Her hand wavered, the hot liquid
splashing on to her bare arm, causing her to stifle a
small sound of pain.

Even as she put down the jug, Daniel was beside
her, holding her scalded arm, frowning down at it as
he hustled her over to the sink and ran cold water
over it.

The scald was only minor—the effect of his fingers
on her skin, the heat of his body standing directly
behind her own so that she only had to lean back to

rest against him and feel the warmth of his breath on her hair, however, were a major threat to her equilibrium and far harder to bear than the sting from the scald.

'I'll spray it with something,' he told her grimly. 'That should take away the sting.'

She had to suppress an insane desire to ask if it would have the same effect on her heart, but stopped herself in time.

This was the Daniel with whom she was familiar. The Daniel who had tended her so comfortingly when she was ill. The Daniel whom she had come to rely on and trust so gradually and insidiously that she hadn't realised until she woke up this morning just how dependent on him she had become.

She wanted him so desperately in her life, she recognised numbly, and not just as a friend. Her heart gave a tremendous bound as she acknowledged her physical need for him. It seemed to jolt visibly right through her body, causing Daniel to tighten his grip on her and demand roughly, 'Are you *sure* you're all right? You've gone as white as snow.'

Driven beyond her self-control, she snapped frantically, 'Will you please stop going on about last night? So you kissed me and I over-reacted. Can't we just leave it at that? It isn't an episode I'm particularly proud of, nor what I feel inclined to sit down and discuss in depth over breakfast, no matter how much *you* seem to relish the thought——'

She broke off as something in the quality of his silence reached her. When she looked at him, he was watching her with a curiously opaque gaze so that she had no idea what he might be thinking.

In a voice totally devoid of any inflexion he told her softly, 'As a matter of fact, I *wasn't* referring to last night.' He looked from her face to the reddening patch on her arm, and immediately her face burned as the realisation that he had been referring to her scald sank in. She took a gulp of her still too hot coffee, badly needing its stimulation and warmth. It burned her throat, making her wince.

'Look, Angelica, while we *are* on the subject of last night...'

Panic churned inside her. She wasn't ready to listen to him—she would never be ready to listen to him on this subject. She could all too easily guess what he wanted to say to her; how he must be determined to ensure that she hadn't misunderstood what had happened, that she wasn't harbouring any foolish illusions about whatever it was that had prompted him to kiss her in the first place, but right at this moment it was more than she was capable of to stand stoically and endure whatever it was he felt he must say to her.

'I want to apologise,' she heard him saying quietly. 'I should never...'

Never have what? Touched her? She suppressed a wild desire to start laughing. Not with amusement. The feeling inside her was more one of frantic hysteria. Hysteria! Her? Impossible!

And yet even knowing that the wise thing, the sensible thing, the only mature thing was to simply stand here and calmly accept whatever it was that he wanted to say to her, she found herself protesting fiercely that there was nothing he needed to say, at the same time, as she edged away from him, putting as much distance between them as she could so that within seconds her back was pressed up against the kitchen unit while he watched her with narrowed, careful eyes.

'Look—what happened last night ... It wasn't important. I—I don't think we need to talk about it. I'm leaving this morning anyway.'

She was starting to gabble with panic and pain, knowing that the only thing that could drive away the agonising ache burning inside her now was for him to come towards her and take her in his arms, to kiss her as he had done last night with tenderness and passion, to assure her that her intense reaction to him was the most exciting thing that had ever happened to him. That he wanted her, that he ...

Her thoughts, that kaleidoscope of mad, whirling, half-formed realisations, suddenly stilled, coalescing into one shimmering, impossible truth. She *wanted* him to love her.

'No.'

The protest came automatically from a throat suddenly raw with tension, past stiff, clumsy lips from which the blood seemed to have drained leaving them oddly numb. Her head was spinning, her heart hammering with panic and shock as she tried to deny the message her emotions were so shockingly giving her. But it wouldn't be denied.

She wanted Daniel to love her. Like a swimmer swept away in a dangerous current, she searched instinctively for something safe to cling to, some reason to logically explain away the impossibility of her thoughts.

It was because of her illness, she told herself hastily and with relief. Yes, that was it, her physical dependence on Daniel during the time of her sickness had fostered a ridiculous and totally unnecessary emotional dependence on him as well and the sooner she was away from him and living on her own again, the faster she would return to normal.

Yes, of course that was it. Once she was no longer living in such a dangerously close proximity to him, things would get back to normal. There was really nothing for her to worry about, for her to panic about. That idiotic surge of agonised fear she had experienced just then...it was just as fictitious as her ridiculous momentary belief that she wanted Daniel to love her. She was behaving like a child—worse than a child.

'Angelica, are you all right?'

The crisp demand made her focus on Daniel's face.

'Yes. Yes, I'm fine,' she assured him, avoiding looking at him. She knew of course that it was impossible for her to have actually fallen in love with him. Things like that didn't happen. At least, not to people like her, people who had learned the hard way the folly of allowing their emotions free rein, of allowing them to rule over more practical and necessary considerations; but even so, it might be wise if she did not actually put her emotions to too stringent a test by looking at him. Not yet at least. In a few days, a week or so, when she had had time to get back to normal, when he had ceased to be a man whom she felt closer to than she had ever felt to any human being, when he had ceased to be a man who turned her bones to liquid and set her body on fire, simply by being in the same room with her, when he had become simply a man who occupied the cottage next to Tom's, a man who had been generous with his time

and his care when she had been in need of them both—
then she would be able to look him directly in the eye.
But not now. No—most definitely not now.

'I think I'll go upstairs and pack up my things,' she
told him shakily, ignoring the fact that she had already
completed this task. 'The sooner I move in next door
and out of your way, the sooner both our lives can
get back to normal.'

She said it with forced cheerfulness, determined not
to allow herself to give way to the despair she could
feel waiting to engulf her if she was foolish enough
to allow it to do so. *If* she was foolish enough to listen
to the agonised, tight little voice inside her which
whispered that it didn't *want* to leave Daniel, that it
wanted to stay here with him forever.

As she hurried out of the kitchen, Daniel watched
her go and muttered grimly under his breath, 'Well,
your life might return to normal, but I'm damn sure
mine won't. You've turned it upside-down with a
vengeance. And to think...'

He grimaced to himself, warning himself mentally
that the worst possible thing he could do now was to
rush her. She was plainly panic-stricken about what
had happened between them last night, and it was obvious to him that there was no way she was anything
like ready to contemplate the kind of commitment *he*
wanted to make with her.

He had come here because he needed space, time
to be alone. The last thing on his mind then had been
romance, the last desire in his life to fall in love. He
shook his head a little at his own folly and tried to
comfort himself with the knowledge that there was
after all no need to rush things, that he had the rest

of the summer here with her. Even so, it was hard to stop himself from going upstairs after her, from taking her in his arms, and letting his emotions, his needs speak for him.

Upstairs Angelica subsided shakily on to the bed. Of course she didn't want Daniel's love, the very idea was ludicrous; so why wasn't she laughing? Why in fact did she feel much closer to tears than laughter? Why did she have this horrible conviction that last night Daniel had been relieved to have an excuse for bringing their lovemaking to an end, if it wasn't because she knew she had totally over-reacted to him? The reason he hadn't stopped her sooner could only be—awful thought—because he had felt sorry for her.

The thought of a man, any man, but especially Daniel making love to her out of pity was so galling, so painful that that pain was actually a physically stabbing sensation within her body, causing her to hug her arms around herself and rock her body slightly as though she was in some way trying to comfort it in its anguish.

She had never felt more confused; her body ached still at its memories of Daniel's touch while her mind ached with the agony of her own folly and her subsequent loss of self-respect, and her heart . . .

Her heart felt nothing, she told herself stubbornly. Nor was she going to allow it to do so.

'Angelica, are you OK?'

The sound of Daniel's voice calling to her from downstairs galvanised her into a flurry of action as she called back breathlessly but determinedly, 'I'm fine—nearly finished.'

She was determined that once she was safely removed to Tom's cottage she would do everything she could do to establish the kind of distance between herself and Daniel which would ensure that he knew that, far from taking his kiss too seriously, she was well aware that it had meant nothing. From now on she would be so cool and indifferent towards him that he would never suspect.

Suspect what?

What was there to suspect, after all, other than that for one weak split second of madness she had actually broken all the rules she had made for herself and allowed herself to yearn for something she could never have? Should never even have wanted. What was the matter with her? She was a modern, independent woman, with a successful business to run, a small circle of good friends, a widowed mother to support and the kind of lifestyle which she knew would probably make her the envy of many a harassed, hard-up young mother with a clutch of children, and a husband who worked so hard that she rarely saw him.

So why had these last few days with Daniel made her feel so aware of a hollowness about her life, a lack of something on which to focus it?

It was the fault of the media, she told herself resentfully, forever pushing on her sex a fictional image of that that was impossible for reality to match. Having it all—career, success, love, children, fulfilment. So many high goals and all of them attainable if only one had the abilities to claim them. Not having it all was a fault, a flaw that lay within the woman herself and must therefore be something she could rectify.

Angry with herself now, Angelica acknowledged that such articles merely fed on her sex's notorious lack of self-worth and that she was surely far too sensible and intelligent to fall for such hype.

And yet she *was* aware of a lack within her life, of a need, call it biological, call it anything you liked. It was there. Wasn't that what had led her into such folly with Giles?

That half-acknowledged desire for a husband, a family.

But she was over that kind of foolishness now. She had learned her lesson. Hadn't she?

CHAPTER SIX

'I THINK that's everything now, thank you.'

They were standing in Tom's kitchen, which was by no means as warm and welcoming as Daniel's.

There was no warm, welcoming Aga here, cosily oozing out its warmth; no comfortable fireside chair, no clean, scrubbed pine table. The room, although it must obviously be the same size as Daniel's, looked smaller, colder, barer, despite the fact that a good deal of its floor space was taken up with a huge, unwieldy dresser filled with a collection of grimy pottery, and what looked like very clumsily put together self-assembly kitchen units with glaringly inappropriate melamine fronts.

Despite her protests, Daniel had insisted on helping Angelica to carry her stuff into Tom's cottage, and now, feeling far more tired than she wanted to admit, she could feel the tension stiffening her spine as she waited for him to go. She suspected that if he stayed much longer she would be in danger of disgracing herself completely and bursting into tears, but for once he seemed immune to her feelings, prowling critically round the kitchen, while she stood by the back door which she was purposefully holding open.

'It seems damp in here. The old boy obviously never got round to having central heating installed. I think we'd better check the bedrooms. The last thing you want right now is a dose of pneumonia.'

The thought of even half a second more in such close intimacy with him provoked such a surge of panic inside her that she snapped back immediately, 'I'm not a child, Daniel, and as for catching pneumonia, that's hardly likely...'

He was looking at her now, frowning with a mixture of surprise and query as he studied her over-flushed face and too bright eyes.

'Are you sure you're up to this?' he asked her quietly. 'There's no disgrace in admitting that you overestimated the extent of your recovery. You could always stay on at my place for a couple more days.'

Her sharp, 'No, I couldn't do that,' caused his frown to deepen, and instinctively Angelica found herself softening her denial by saying jerkily, 'I've imposed on you for long enough... Intruding on your privacy.'

'That's hardly your fault. You couldn't help being ill.'

'Well, it's kind of you, but now that I'm here I might as well stay. The place probably just needs airing.'

'Mm. Well, if you're sure. I'll just carry your case upstairs for you, shall I?'

'No—no, it's all right. I can manage.'

She was still holding the door open, and she could tell from the way he looked from her tight face to the open door that he knew of her anxiety for him to go.

He confirmed it by saying unexpectedly, 'It's all right, Angelica. I'm going, but remember, if you *do* need me for anything, anything at all...'

Was it her imagination or did his gaze really linger for a second on her mouth, causing her to remember how eagerly she had pleaded with him last night for his possession of it? That fear was enough to make her say fiercely, 'Thank you. I'm sure there won't be.'

He was almost level with her now. Another few seconds and he would be gone and she would be able to breathe properly again, but just as he started to walk past her he stopped, looking down at her, so that she was virtually imprisoned between his body and the door.

As he bent his head, she had a startled second in which to recognise that he actually intended to kiss her.

Automatically she stepped back, panic-stricken at the thought of having his mouth touching her skin, terrified of what that contact might do to her fragile self-control. After last night her belief in her own ability to control her physical responsiveness to him was completely shattered.

She saw surprise and then something that might have been pain or which might have been anger cloud his eyes, before he put up his hand. Jerking back from it, she banged her head painfully against the door, wincing as her eyes stung with tears. She closed them quickly, so that she didn't see the concern in Daniel's as he took hold of her, his long fingers expertly probing beneath the softness of her hair to investigate the damage to her scalp. Roughly he told her, 'You little fool! What did you think I was going to do to you?'

'Nothing.'

The lie was muffled and indistinct, primarily because, as he searched to make sure she hadn't broken the skin, Daniel had closed the gap between them and pushed her head against his shoulder so that she now couldn't move, couldn't even breathe without becoming affected by the warm male scent of him, so powerfully familiar to her senses now that her whole body was already reacting to it as though it were a familiar and intensely powerful aphrodisiac.

She tried to breathe in deeply to calm her agitated senses and then realised unsteadily that she had done exactly the wrong thing, just as Daniel contradicted curtly, 'Liar. You thought I was going to kiss you, didn't you?'

Why did he have this penchant for asking questions which would have far better been left unraised? Another man, a more tactful man, a more cowardly man perhaps, would have known why she had ducked out of the way, but would not have asked her why.

'Certainly not,' she denied untruthfully.

'And if I had been?'

Her heart was fluttering frantically. The need to flick her tongue over her dry lips was unbearable, but a wisdom she hadn't known she possessed screamed at her to resist the temptation.

What was he trying to do? Find out perhaps just how vulnerable she was to him, so that he could firmly make it clear that her desire was not reciprocated? He was honest enough and strong-willed enough to do so, but her pride wouldn't allow her to be manipulated in that kind of way, especially when she was very much afraid that if he did kiss her she was just as capable this morning of acting as idiotically uncontrollably as she had done last night.

'But you hadn't been,' she insisted shakily and stubbornly. 'After all, why should you? We don't have that kind of—of relationship.'

He was still holding on to her but she had managed to lift her face away from his body and focus on a point over his left shoulder.

'Well, you're going to have a nasty bruise under your hair,' he told her rather more grimly than she thought necessary. 'But the skin isn't broken. I suppose there isn't much point in reiterating that if you *do* discover that you aren't as fully recovered as you believe your bed is still there. You're far too independent to admit it, even if you did.'

Independent? Her? She grimaced mirthlessly to herself. If only he knew it, she would give almost anything to have him sweep her off her feet and tell her passionately and firmly that he wasn't going to let her go and that her place was by his side.

That knowledge made her want to weep inside for her own vulnerability and folly. That kind of behaviour belonged to a Georgette Heyer romance, not real life. She tried mentally to equate her belief that men and women should coexist on equal terms with this hitherto unsuspected streak of blatant weakness which suggested treacherously to her that there might on occasion be something to be said for a man who, while acknowledging a woman's right to determine her own life and make her own decisions, also knew that there were times when, while 'no' most certainly did not mean 'yes', and that on no account did any woman want to be forced to accept something that was unacceptable to her, she might not be totally averse to being taken in a man's arms and told that he loved and wanted her, no matter how much she might seem not to want to hear those words. But then that of course presupposed that the man concerned *did* love her in the first place. That he was not simply conducting a cold-blooded experiment, designed to show him how vulnerable she might be to him.

'If you're *sure* you can manage on your own,' Daniel was saying now as he stepped slowly back from her, almost as though he was actually reluctant to leave, a traitorous thought suggested.

She ignored it determinedly and said firmly, 'Of course I can... I'm an adult, Daniel, not a child.'

And yet the moment he had gone, she had an insane desire to call him back to tell him she had changed her mind, to tell him that she didn't want to live alone here in Tom's cottage when she could be sharing his roof, his company, his bed.

Angry with herself, she closed the door firmly behind her and then turned around to survey her new domain.

She wrinkled her nose as she smelled the stale, damp air of the kitchen, and glanced around the uninspiring room without enthusiasm. She'd better explore the rest of the house. Normally her surroundings were not something which particularly bothered her. Her house in London, which she had bought fully furnished, was convenient and small and she was not particularly attached to it. After all, she spent more time at her office than she did at home.

She supposed if she had an ideal of what a home should be it would be something comfortable and slightly rambling with a huge garden. The kind of house that needed a large family to bring it to life.

'Stop it,' she warned herself grimly.

The house proved to be depressingly unappealing. The sitting-room was furnished with a worn square of carpet and the kind of heavy, old-fashioned furniture that always looked ugly. There was a small fireplace, clumsily boarded up with a two-bar electric fire set in front of it. Thin curtains hung at the window.

Upstairs was very much the same. The cottage was depressing, Angelica recognised, all the more so because Tom had confided in her that his uncle had not been a poor man, but had for some reason been obsessed with being very careful with his money. To such an extent obviously that he had refused to allow himself any kind of material comfort.

She chose the smaller of the two bedrooms simply because it was furthest away from the party-wall with Daniel's cottage. The cottages were stone-built and the walls far too solid for any sound to travel through from one to the other, but even so she felt she would sleep a little better without the knowledge that Daniel was sleeping only feet away from her.

Fortunately the cottage had an immersion heater which she immediately switched on before grimly removing what would be her bedding from the cupboard. The only way she was going to sleep in these cold, damp sheets was after she had taken them to the nearest launderette and washed and aired them. That meant a drive to Aberystwyth, but perhaps that was just as well. At least it would take her away from Daniel for several hours.

She was just on her way back downstairs when she heard someone knocking on the door. Knowing that it could only be Daniel, she had a cowardly urge to simply stay where she was and ignore him. But of course he knew she was in here.

When she opened the door, he had his back to it. He turned round quickly and her heart did a complete somersault.

'I'm just going to the farm. I wondered if you wanted to come with me. I could introduce you to Mrs Davies.'

She thought quickly. She could leave for Aberystwyth while he was at the farm, and that way she could avoid any awkward questions he might choose to ask her about her fitness to drive. And if she refused his offer it would surely reinforce the fact that she had no intentions of trespassing into his life now that she had moved out of his cottage.

'No, thanks,' she told him, avoiding looking at him as she saw him start to frown.

'Angelica, I *know* how you feel about your independence, but——'

'I'm grateful to you for all you've done for me, Daniel,' she interrupted him huskily. 'But I'm fine now and I don't want——'

'Any more interference in your life from me,' he supplied for her. She heard the anger in his voice and bit her lip. She did sound very ungrateful and selfish, but what else could she do? She already knew that he was a man of deep compassion and responsibility, but if he genuinely couldn't see how dangerously emotionally involved with him she was getting, then it had to be up to her to keep the contact between them to a minimum, even if that meant offending him.

Perhaps after all she had been wrong about him guessing how much her passionate response to him last night had revealed. Maybe in the circles in which he moved such passion was common currency and unimportant. And yet she would not have thought it of him. He was a sexually experienced man, but not one whom she would have thought took such relationships lightly.

What could she say? She looked at him and wished she hadn't when she saw the unmistakable glitter of anger in his eyes. He had every right to be annoyed with her. On the surface at least her behaviour was churlish in the extreme. But for both their sakes the last thing he could possibly want was the embarrassment of having her become too dependent on him, of having her fall in love with him.

She felt her heart freeze, all her muscles clenching in protest at what she was thinking. She couldn't do that. She must not do it.

Somehow she managed to say shakily, 'I—I think it best if we live our own separate lives from now on. It's not that I'm not grateful to you for everything you've done, but sometimes—well, sometimes that kind of intimacy can foster—can give rise to—to problems that neither of us would want. Of course if there's any way I can repay you for all that you've done for me...'

She could see how much she had angered him, and beneath the anger in the depths of his eyes she could have sworn she saw a momentary stark pain that made her own emotions jolt in aching response. She was imagining it, she told herself ten minutes later as she watched from upstairs while he walked down the track that led to the farm, a solitary and somehow lonely figure, who walked with a limp which somehow seemed to have become slightly more pronounced. His head was bowed slightly as though in defeat, as though her refusal to go with him had actually hurt him.

Don't be a fool, she derided herself. You're looking for things you want to see. If he'd felt anything for you, anything at all, he would have told you so last night. Her heart gave another frightened jolt as she realised how quickly she had gone from the devastating revelation that she wanted far more from him than his clinical concern for another human being, to the actual acknowledgement of how important he had become to her. So important that without him...

Without him what? Nothing! That was what, she told herself stoutly as she collected her bag and her car keys and picked up her laundry.

Aberystwyth was busier than she had expected. She had trouble finding a launderette, and she discovered shakily that she was by no means as fully recovered as she had believed, and then, on her way back to the car, for no logical reasons that she could think of, she found herself stopping outside a small off-licence dithering about whether or not she could perhaps buy Daniel a bottle of good wine as a token 'thank-you' for all that he had done for her. Perhaps she could even make him a meal. It would after all only be a reciprocal gesture for the meal he had made her last night. Not even the sternest critic could read into such a gesture any hint that she was deliberately trying to foster some kind of intimacy between them. Indeed, one might say that the least she could do to thank him was to offer him some return hospitality. So why was she hesitating, wondering not so much if he might misconstrue her motives, but whether she was being totally honest with herself about them? Was she already weakening from her decision this morning to treat him as nothing more than a casual acquaintance, someone who would soon be gone from her life and on no account someone she could allow herself to become too involved with?

In the end, after much hesitation and because she could see she was attracting attention from inside the shop, she went inside and purchased a bottle of wine.

On the way back to her car, she passed a fishmonger's displaying live lobsters, which made her shudder a little even though she enjoyed their flesh. Seeing the crustaceans clawing angrily in their captivity somehow or other put her off eating them.

Instead she bought some salmon, which she realised almost immediately was a mistake, since her cottage did not possess a fridge, which meant she would have to ask Daniel if she could use his.

She flushed angrily, reflecting that it would serve her right if he did accuse her of deliberately trying to foster an intimacy between them. Surely it was one of the oldest feminine wiles in the book, on a par with begging for his help with some trivial practical task, such as unblocking a blocked sink.

She looked at the salmon and, cursing herself under her breath, grimly returned to her car with her purchases and her laundry, depositing them there before setting out to find somewhere selling domestic appliances.

Eventually she found an appropriate shop, and luckily they had in stock a small fridge-freezer, which she hoped would fit in the back of her car.

Eventually it did, although the shop owner, plainly not used to the immediacy of a city dweller's desires, could not understand why she preferred to take the appliance with her rather than wait a week for him to deliver it, and Angelica had no intention of explaining to him.

The salmon had turned out to be a very expensive purchase indeed, she reflected wrathfully as she set out for her return journey, thankful to see that Daniel did not appear to be about as she parked her car outside the cottage.

It took her almost fifteen minutes to manoeuvre the fridge-freezer into the kitchen and clear a space for it, by which time she was both sticky and out of breath, as well as out of temper. To discover that she had also committed the cardinal sin of forgetting to buy a plug was almost the last straw. How could *she*, who prided herself on her practicality, have been so stupid? Because she had been thinking not about what she was doing but *why* she was doing it, that was why. Because in short she had been thinking about Daniel. Because, although she would no doubt attempt to deny it to herself, the entire exercise from start to finish had been nothing more than a bout of stupid self-indulgence, allowing herself to think about Daniel under the guise of behaving in a way that was both logical and necessary. Well, she *might* have been stupid enough to allow herself that self-deceit, but now it was over. An expensive mistake, she admitted ruefully, staring helplessly at the gleaming white box now dominating the kitchen . . . and totally useless.

She would have to go all the way back to Aberystwyth for a plug, something she simply did not have the energy to do right now, which meant—which meant that the most sensible thing she could do was to cook the salmon and then take a portion of it round to Daniel for him to eat on his own . . . Which was what she should have thought of doing in the first place, instead of making elaborate plans to entertain him.

Flushed with exertion and mortification, she was still standing glowering at the fridge when Daniel suddenly walked in through the open kitchen door, demanding grittily, 'Where the hell have you been?'

At the sound of his voice, she whirled round, shock widening her eyes, confusion stilling her tongue as she stared at him in open-mouthed astonishment.

He frowned as he saw the fridge and then demanded, 'How did that thing get in here?'

'On its own two feet,' Angelica suggested sarcastically as her shock receded. The last thing she needed now was Daniel here to witness her idiocy, and just to make sure that she stuck by her original decision not to allow any further intimacy between them she added for good measure, 'There's a parcel on the dresser for you. Some salmon I got in Aberystwyth. A small thank-you for all your—your hospitality.'

His look of biting incredulity made her wince. 'Some *salmon*?'

'And—and a bottle of wine,' she added defensively. 'So——'

'Some salmon and a bottle of wine . . . I take it that I'm intended to enjoy these—gifts on my own.'

His obvious anger was beginning to unnerve her. What on earth had she done? Perhaps she *was* being a little ungracious, too offhand—the last thing she wanted to do was to make him feel she hadn't appreciated everything he had done for her.

'Well, I *had* intended to cook it for you,' she heard herself saying, weakening. 'Only . . .' She stopped and gestured helplessly towards the fridge before she could stop herself, tensing as he stepped closer to it to inspect it.

'You carried this thing in here by yourself, I take it,' he asked her with apparent mildness.

Taken off guard, relieved that he hadn't yet noticed that it had no plug, she nodded and was stunned to hear him saying fiercely, 'You little fool. How often do you have to be reminded that you've just been through an extremely debilitating illness? What the hell do you think would have happened if you'd collapsed?'

'I could have damaged the fridge,' she suggested, tongue in cheek.

'*I* was thinking more of the damage you could have caused yourself,' he cautioned her acidly.

'Well, I didn't collapse, so you needn't worry that you're about to have me back on your hands,' she told him caustically, praying that he wouldn't guess how much she wanted to read far more than he could have intended into his apparent concern.

'And now, if you don't mind, I'd like to get this fridge installed and working,' she added for good measure, determined to get him out of her kitchen before the odd weakness she could feel in her legs had her fainting in his arms like a Victorian heroine.

'Fine. Well, I'll put the plug on it for you, shall I? Where is it?'

'I'm perfectly capable of putting on my own plug,' Angelica told him wildly, trying to reject his offer; but he was already frowning as he looked round the kitchen as though searching for something. His frown was giving way to something approaching amusement as he turned back to her and, folding his arms across his chest, said provocatively,

'Really? Well, go on, then.'

Go on, then. If only she could.

'All in my own good time. And now if you'd just like to leave me alone——'

'You haven't got a plug, have you?' he challenged directly.

Angelica gaped at him. Damn him. She might have known he would guess... but it was only a guess—for all he knew the plug could still be in her car. She tilted her chin and eyed him balefully, wondering if she dared risk refuting his claim.

'You forgot to buy the plug, didn't you?'

He was actually laughing at her. How dared he? Anyone could make a mistake—and it was all his fault anyway. If it hadn't been for him, for needing to repay him, she wouldn't even have bought the damn thing in the first place.

'So what if I have? I can go back to Aberystwyth tomorrow and buy one. The only reason I bought it anyway was so that——'

She broke off, biting her lip, as her gaze fell betrayingly on the parcel of salmon.

He watched her, his own eyes suddenly narrowing speculatively. 'You bought it because of that,' he demanded, looking at the salmon. 'What the hell for, when you know damn well I've got a perfectly adequate fridge next door?'

'I didn't want to be beholden to you,' Angelica told him stiffly.

'Beholden,' he repeated incredulously.

She tensed as he unfolded his arms and came purposefully towards her.

'If I wasn't so damn sure that you're already so weak that you can barely stand, I think I'd shake you until your teeth rattled. Independence is fine, but you're carrying it too far. You could have asked me——'

'Perhaps I could have, but maybe I didn't *want* to,' she interrupted him dangerously, her emotions fighting with logic and common sense as she ached to give in to the insidious pull he exerted on her senses.

There was a small, telling pause and then he said quietly—too quietly, 'I see. And can I ask why—or shall I guess? This determination to make it clear to me that you no longer want any kind of intimacy between us wouldn't have anything to do with last night, would it?'

He *was* angry now, really angry. She could see it in his eyes, hear it in his voice.

'Nothing at all,' she lied as firmly as she could. He was looking right at her, and she forced herself to hold his gaze without wavering as she added with a small shrug, 'Why should it have? It was only a kiss.'

There was a brief, dangerous silence when she couldn't bear to look at him any longer. He ought to be relieved that she was behaving so sensibly, not standing there glowering at her, looking at her as though he would in fact like to take hold of her and shake her as he had threatened.

'Only a kiss, was it?' he said grittily at last. 'Well, as I remember it, it was far more than only a kiss, but since I should hate to contradict a lady I'll have to accept your version of events, won't I?'

He was gone before she could speak, slamming the door behind him with a force that made the window rattle.

She stared after him in astonishment. She had never seen him come close to losing his temper before, and yet after all what had she said, what had she done to provoke such anger? What had he wanted her to say— that last night in his arms she had experienced something so close to emotional and physical ecstasy that the memory of it would stay with her for the rest of her life, coming between her and any chance she might have had of finding happiness with another man? Of course not.

She stared at the fridge and found that it was turning from something solid into something insubstantial as a jelly. She was crying, she recognised, crying over a stupid, stubborn man who couldn't see when a woman was doing her best to protect him from the effects of her own foolishness.

He didn't deserve her consideration. He didn't deserve anything at all from her... Coming in here, bullying her, shouting at her, making her cry. Refusing her salmon and her wine, she added wrathfully, seeing them still on the dresser and heaping coals on the fire of her anger. Well, *she* didn't care. Their quarrel was probably the best thing that could have happened for both their sakes. So why did she feel as though the sky had suddenly fallen in on her? Why indeed!

CHAPTER SEVEN

IN HIS own cottage, Daniel paced restlessly around his kitchen, until the ache in his torn muscles forced him to stop and massage his injured leg.

He oughtn't to have let things get so out of hand. He ought not to have challenged her at all, in fact. He *knew* her past, how wary she was of emotional commitment. He frowned as he stared out of the window, torn between going back and laying his cards on the table, telling her how he felt about her, and fearing that it was still much too soon; that if he did so, she would reject him out of hand and then firmly shut him out of her life.

If only he weren't committed to going to Cardiff first thing in the morning... But this appointment with his specialist had been made months ago when he had first been told that the only way for him to give his body time to recover was either for the specialist to appoint someone to physically restrain him from overworking, or for him to take himself off somewhere where it would be impossible for him to do so.

He had chosen the latter course, and, reluctant though he had been to admit it, the enforced freedom from stress had had the desired effect. All he needed now was for his specialist to confirm what he already knew in his own mind, that his torn muscles were beginning to heal, just as he knew that his stubborn subconscious was finally beginning to give up its burden of bitterness and guilt. The past was something over which he had no control. He had told himself that for a long time, but it was only over these last few weeks that he had finally come to accept it and find some peace of mind.

Perhaps if he were to talk to Angelica, tell her that he too... But no. He couldn't lay the burden of his problems on *her* shoulders, not when she already had so many of her own.

He wished he weren't having to leave her on her own. He had asked them at the farm to keep an eye on the cottages while he was away.

He had other business in Cardiff besides visiting his specialist. Business which would keep him in the city for at least a couple of days.

Odd to think that it was Angelica who had finally enabled him to come to the decision he had been putting off making for all these months, torn between his own needs, and those of his almost overwhelming burden of guilt and responsibility. But now his decision was made.

He was not after all his father, and in his heart he knew that his father would never have wanted him to sacrifice his own emotional needs in order to devote his life to something which had been his father's creation rather than his own. Yes, he was going to be very busy while in Cardiff, but never so busy that Angelica would not be there with him every second of his time, if only in the deepest privacy of his own thoughts.

For almost an hour after Daniel had gone, Angelica could only go slowly and shakily through the motions of living. He had been so angry with her, and yet strangely neither at the time, nor now, when she thought about it, had that anger been threatening or frightening. Rather it had been challenging, invigorating almost—certainly it had aroused within her a reckless responsiveness which she could scarcely recognise as belonging to her own personality.

Uncomfortably she admitted that it was almost as though a part of her had actually *enjoyed* challenging him, had actually wanted...

What? To be dragged into his arms and kissed with the kind of passion which would sweep away the barriers of her self-restraint without her having to make a conscious decision?

She made a small moue of distaste. She had always semi-despised the kind of woman who did not have the courage to make her own decisions and then to stand by them, and yet here she was practically admitting that if Daniel *had* chosen to react in the kind of dominant male manner that surely had no place in any relationship between two modern adults, she would almost have welcomed it. She was becoming obsessed with the man and with how she felt about him. This was what came of having too much time on her hands; perhaps the mere fact that she was spending so much time thinking about Daniel was a sign that she ought to go back to London. For the sake of her emotional sanity if nothing else.

She went to bed early, reminding herself that this was after all what she was here in Wales for—plenty of rest and relaxation, and besides, there was no incentive to stay up when there was no Daniel to spend the evening with. She missed him, felt lonely without

him, found herself about to turn round and make
some comment to him, and was appalled to discover
how easily and quickly she had slipped into the habit
of becoming used to having him there. It was only
now that she was on her own that she recognised how
much of a stimulating challenge living with him had
been.

Living with him. As sleep claimed her, she trembled
inwardly, not wanting to slide into sleep with that
thought clinging to her mind, frightened of the images
it might release to torment her dreams, but knowing
she could do nothing to stop them.

It was the sound of something rattling against her
window that woke her. At first she thought it was
rain, very heavy rain, but then as the sleep cleared
from her brain she realised that the noise was too intense and too spasmodic. It was...it was stones—
someone was throwing stones up at her window.

Without thinking of the danger, she pushed back
the duvet and hurried over to the window, astonished
to see Daniel standing on the lawn below, frowning
up at her. Their quarrel was forgotten, as she hurried
quickly downstairs to let him in, knowing that something must be wrong for him to have wakened her.

It was still so early that the air was cold enough to
turn to vapour as Daniel breathed. As she held open
the door, he brought into the kitchen with him the
cold, clean scent of the early morning, tinged with
the salt smell of the sea.

The coldness of the morning made her shiver as she
asked him anxiously, 'What is it? What's wrong?' As
she closed the door she glanced at her watch and saw

that it was only half-past five. No wonder she felt as though she had been woken in the middle of the night. No wonder it felt so chilly outside. Panic raced through her nervous system, cramping her stomach and increasing her heartbeat. Something must be dreadfully wrong for Daniel to be here like this. Was the bug she had had contagious? Her brain felt like glue, her body heavy and clumsy as she tried to come fully awake.

'It's my car,' she heard Daniel saying flatly. 'The damn coil's gone.'

His car? She stared at him in disbelief. He had woken her up like that at half-past five in the morning to tell her that about his car!

She paused in the automatic habit of making coffee. 'Your car——'

'It won't start,' he told her brusquely, 'and I've got to be in Cardiff for nine. I was wondering . . . Could I borrow yours?'

He had come round here at this time in the morning because he wanted to borrow her car?

'I'll be gone for a couple of days,' he told her, apparently unaware of her silence. 'I wouldn't ask, but this appointment with the specialist is something I daren't miss, and there's no phone here for me to ring him and try to change it.'

Neither cottage possessed a telephone, but Angelica had stopped listening to his explanations after she had heard the word specialist. She had often wondered about his injury, but had not liked to ask what had caused it. Now she queried impetuously, 'A specialist?' remembering how the local doctor had

commented to her that Daniel was very familiar wit
all the unpleasant physical indignities of illness.

Normally Daniel hated discussing the accident wit
anyone, but Angelica was different, and, even mo
important, for the first time she was actually e
pressing curiosity about him, actually *showing* th
she wanted to know something about him, that sh
was concerned for him.

'Yes,' he told her gently, taking the coffee-jug fo
her and filling it with water. 'Six months ago he tol
me that unless I slowed down and gave my muscle
time to heal, I'd be left with a permanent injury. H
convinced me enough to make me look round fo
somewhere close enough to Cardiff for me to be o
hand if necessary, but also remote enough for me t
give my muscles a chance to recover. My father ha
always been particularly fond of this part of Wales
so I drove down here, saw the cottage, discovered tha
it was empty and arranged to rent it.'

'Cardiff... is that where your home is?' Angelic
asked him slowly. So he *wasn't* a local. He *didn't* liv
here permanently as she had at first assumed.

'In a manner of speaking, although for the last fiv
years, at one time or another, I've lived in Milan, Ne
York, London and Paris. My father owned and ra
a small and very highly specialised company pro
ducing very advanced electronics. I ran the sales sid
of the business. The idea was that, when he even
tually retired, I would take over as managing directo
and that he would become our technical consultant
Unfortunately fate had other ideas. My father was
workaholic; I think perhaps after my mother died, h
turned his attention more and more to his work as

means of coping with his grief. He was never very good at talking about his feelings, although as a child I grew up knowing that he loved me and feeling very secure in that love. The problem was that once I was adult I began to see certain flaws in my father's lifestyle, and he on his part couldn't always understand why I refused to devote myself one hundred and fifty per cent to the business in the same way that he had.

'I tried to tell him that I wanted much more from life than a successful company. We quarrelled about it. He was working on a new invention, testing it out in our laboratories. He liked to work there alone at night after all the others had gone home. What went wrong we'll never really know. All I *do* know is that I suddenly had this need to see him. I was due to fly back to New York in the morning. I drove down to the factory. When I got there I could see the flames through the windows of the lab. The night-watchman had already rung for the fire brigade. He hadn't realised my father was inside.

'I tried to get him out...but the heat, the smoke... I must have collapsed. They told me later that I'd acted like a fool, imperilling the lives of the men who'd rescued me as well as my own, and that my father had probably died from asphyxiation within minutes of the fire's starting, that I couldn't have done a thing to help him. I tore my leg muscles when I tried to get in through one of the windows.

'It doesn't matter how many times I tell myself that I wasn't to blame; the guilt remains, the feeling that I could have done something, that I ought to have done something—at least until recently. Now—now,

I think I'm finally coming to terms with the fact that I'm not omnipotent.'

He had stopped speaking. The room was silent, apart from the soft burble of the coffee-machine as the water filtered over the coffee.

Angelica tried to speak and found that she couldn't because her throat was blocked by a huge lump of compassion and understanding.

It overwhelmed her to realise how much that he was leaving unsaid, she automatically sensed and understood. She too knew the burden of responsibility that came with taking over a business built up by a much-loved parent, but in Daniel's case how much harder that burden must have been to assume, feeling as he so obviously did that he was in some way at fault for not having prevented his father's death, for not having been there to help him when he most needed help. Yes, she could understand his feelings, could understand and share them so much, in fact, that the intensity of her awareness of all that he must have suffered made her want to retreat from him and from the knowledge of her own emotional responsiveness to him. It frightened her, this intensity, this need to go to him and hold him, to offer him her compassion, her understanding, her love. She shivered, her feet and arms cold, realising suddenly that all she was wearing was her nightdress.

Daniel in contrast was dressed for his journey to the city in clean jeans, and one of the checked shirts he seemed to favour and which as she well knew felt so soft against the skin. Over it he was wearing a dark green sweater warm enough to keep off the early morning chill.

Her eyes burned with tears, as she suddenly saw him, not as he was now, but inert, a vulnerable crumpled figure, choking on the poisonous smoke that enveloped him, trying desperately to reach a man who was already gone beyond all human help. She shivered again, but this time not with the cold. Daniel saw it and frowned.

She was so quiet. He had no idea what she was thinking, what she was feeling. She seemed so remote from him, so distant, while he on the other hand felt so open and vulnerable to her that her very silence was almost an act of rejection.

What had he expected, what had he wanted, what had he hoped for—that she would open her arms to him, and embrace him as he had so often longed to be held as a child? That she would hold him and kiss him and tell him that he would never again have to be alone, that she would always be with him, share his life with him? He made a sound of angry self-disgust deep in his throat. He was behaving like a fool. He had already warned himself not to rush her, and yet here he was burdening her with the kind of emotional outburst which common sense told him would make her withdraw from him almost as fast as his lovemaking had done.

Angelica heard the sound and it jerked her back to reality. So Daniel had told her about his father; so he had allowed her to see what he had suffered. She would be a fool to read too much into it. He had told her most likely because his visit to the specialist had brought it sharply into focus in his mind, and perhaps because he wanted her to understand just why he needed to borrow her car. If she allowed herself to believe there was any other reason, to imagine that there was any personal message in his confidences . . . Turning her back on him, she walked across the kitchen and picked up her car keys.

'I'm afraid there's only half a tank of petrol,' she warned him as she gave them to him. 'You'll have to fill the tank.'

'No problem, mine only had a couple of gallons in it anyway, and naturally I'll replace whatever I use.'

He was so formal now, so distant. The time for confidences was over, that was plain.

She gestured towards the coffee and asked him abruptly, 'Would you like a cup? It's ready now.'

He glanced at his watch, an expensive watch, she realised now, not the kind of watch a man who earned his living from a little fishing and a little farm labouring would ever be able to afford.

'Yes, if you don't mind. I got in such a panic when my car wouldn't start, that I didn't bother making myself a drink.'

'Will it take long to get to Cardiff?' she asked him as she poured their coffee, the question one she would have asked any casual acquaintance. And that was after all what they were, she told herself firmly.

'Not really. I could see the specialist and be back by mid-afternoon, if I didn't have this other business to attend to.' He frowned and put down his coffee-mug. 'I don't really like leaving you alone here without any form of transport. I'll try to keep my trip as short as I can. If you need help of any kind, there's the farm, but that's a fair walk away and——'

'I'm fully recovered now, and certainly capable of walking a mile or so if necessary,' Angelica told him crisply.

She didn't want to hear the concern in his voice. It weakened her too much . . . made her too aware of her lonely, stupid, emotional responsiveness to him . . .

Just to hear that undertone of concern in his voice made such a *frisson* of sensation run through her that she had to turn her back on him in case he saw the betraying reaction of her body. Under her nightdress she could feel the sharp stiffening of her nipples and the corresponding coiling tension that gripped her lower body.

Behind her she heard the sound of the coffee-mug being placed on the work-top and knew that he was standing up, that soon he would be gone.

'I'm sorry I had to disturb you so early,' she heard him saying, and knew that he was walking towards her. 'I'm very grateful to you for loaning me your car. I promise I'll take good care of it.'

'It's the least I can do after all that you've done for me,' she responded in a low voice, not daring to turn round, knowing that he was standing right behind her.

What did he *want*? He already had the keys. There was nothing else she could give him. But it seemed *he* thought there was. She tensed as she felt his hands on her shoulders, his breath warm and frighteningly arousing against her skin as he asked almost uncertainly, 'A good-luck kiss would be very much appreciated.'

A good-luck *kiss*. Perhaps it was the sort of thing any man would say in such circumstances. The trouble was she wasn't familiar enough with the kind of intimacy they had shared to know how a man might react.

Certainly it was true that on a handful of occasions she and Tom had exchanged fraternal kisses of good luck. Kisses given and taken in the spirit of true non-sexual friendship, and that on those occasions she had always appreciated his warmth and concern, the physical evidence of the friendship she knew he felt towards her.

But to kiss Daniel in that way, Daniel whose mere presence behind her was enough to make her emotions go completely out of control; if she turned round now and kissed him . . . She felt herself tremble and yet did nothing to resist when he slowly turned her round and then looked gravely into her eyes, so intently that she felt as though he was searching there for something. Her heart had started to pound so frantically she felt sure he must be aware of what she was feeling and why, but his hands still slid slowly into her hair, caressing her scalp, smoothing away some of its tension. She couldn't help it; all her concentration focused on his mouth, on knowing that soon it would touch hers, on knowing that when it did . . . She touched her tongue-tip to her own lips in an unintentionally betraying gesture, her body trembling as he made a very male and erotic sound of satisfaction in response.

'Wish me luck,' he whispered softly against her mouth, gently rubbing his lips with hers, the warm pressure of his words sensitising her so that she sighed in tremulous eagerness as his mouth caressed hers, gently nibbling at it, coaxing it into clinging responsiveness so that she forgot how she had come to be in his arms in the first place and knew only how much she wanted to be there. How much she wanted the pleasure of this delirious physical contact of mouth against mouth, of his tongue-tip stroking against her half-parted lips, and then far less gently moving in rhythmic urgency against her own, reinforcing the sudden hardness of his body as his hands moulded her scalp, holding her still beneath the sudden flaring of passion that engulfed them both.

She wanted him, Angelica recognised despairingly. She wanted him so much that if he picked her up now and carried her back to bed . . .

She gave a tiny shudder, and abruptly Daniel released her. Her face stung with hot colour, as she wondered if he had guessed what she was thinking, if he had recognised that while for him that urgent, fierce passion had simply been born of their physical proximity, for her it had its roots in something much more complex and dangerous.

She wasn't going to use the word love. She dared not allow herself to use it, dared not allow herself to admit it into her vocabulary. Not so very long ago after all she had told herself she loved another and very different man. A man who had deceived her, lied to her, cheated on her.

She shivered and tried to step back from him only to discover that Daniel had one hand tangled in her hair.

'You're cold,' he said in sudden concern, frowning down at her. 'I should have realised before.'

His frown deepened as he saw that her feet were bare beneath the hem of her nightdress.

'You should still be in bed, not standing down here in the freezing cold. That's my fault.'

He was still looking at her and she had to fight to stop herself from crossing her arms protectively over her breasts to conceal from him the betraying hardness of her nipples as she prayed that he would mistake her arousal for cold.

As he released her, he rested his free hand against the curve of her waist, unintentionally dragging the fabric of her nightdress tight across her breasts. She froze immediately, sensing the sudden concentration of his attention on her breasts.

Suddenly she wanted—needed to draw air deeply into her lungs, but didn't dare. If he were to raise his hand to touch her breasts now, to delicately run his fingertip around the urgent crowns of flesh pressing so eagerly against the soft cotton, if he were to follow up that exploratory caress with the moist softness of his tongue... She felt the heat burn through her body, a heat which had nothing to do with any outer change of temperature but which was instead generated and fuelled purely by her own thoughts and desires.

'You're going to be late,' she told him huskily, forcing herself to step back from him.

For a moment his fingers tightened on her waist as though he was reluctant to let her go, as though the same thoughts burning through her were echoed within him, and then slowly, reluctantly almost he responded.

'Yes. Yes, I'd better make a start.'

And she was free to turn her back on him and walk away from him, busying herself with their empty mugs, trying to behave as though she was no more aware of him as a man than had he been her father or Tom.

She heard him walking towards the door, slowly almost as though he didn't really want to go. She ached to turn round and run to him, to wrap him in her arms and tell him not to be afraid.

Which was about the most stupid thought she had ever had. Even if he was apprehensive about his consultation, he would scarcely thank her for mentioning it. She wanted to ask him when he would be back, as though knowing would give her a goal to wait for. Her heart missed a beat as she swallowed on that betraying need. She was allowing him to become far too important to her. Far, far too important.

As he reached the door, Daniel paused. He ached to turn round and go back to her, to sweep her up in his arms and tell her how much he wanted her, how much he needed her, to beg her to come with him.

She had responded so sweetly to him when he kissed her, until she'd realised how aroused he was. He cursed himself under his breath. What was the point in telling himself that he must not rush her when he then went and did exactly the opposite?

As he opened the door, he forced himself to say as casually as he could, 'Thanks again for loaning me your car, Angelica.'

'You're welcome.' She dared not go towards him in case he read in her eyes all that she was trying so desperately to deny.

As he opened the door and walked out, she ached to tell him that she'd be thinking about him.

* * *

For a long time after he had gone, she sat in her cold, empty kitchen forcing herself to admit the unwanted truth. She loved Daniel in a way that made her laugh at the shallowness of the emotion she had once thought she felt for Giles and which she had so misguidedly given the same name. There was no comparison between them. No way in which the way she had felt about Giles could ever come within a million miles of reaching the intensity and complexity of emotions she now acknowledged she felt and didn't want to feel for Daniel.

Without him time dragged, and it appalled her that she, who had not only been quite content to spend time on her own, but had actually relished it, hoarding it away like a miser with gold, to be enjoyed stealthily and almost guiltily when she was on her own, should now feel such a burden of aloneness, such an intensity of need for one specific other human being, that time itself actually seemed to stand still.

The weather was glorious, tempting her to find her way down on to the beach so that she could lie in the warmth of the sun and watch her city-pale skin taking on a golden peachy glow. With the small cove to herself and no one to see her, she quickly lost all self-consciousness and found herself quite easily dispensing with the rather staid one-piece swimsuit which she had thrown into her suitcase at the last minute.

She even ventured as far as the farm, and lingered once she was there, not so much because she wanted Mrs Davies's company but because the farmer's wife was so easily induced to talk about Daniel whom it quickly became plain she greatly admired.

It quite shocked Angelica to discover how much it meant to her to find that Mrs Davies had no idea what had brought him to this quiet corner of the Pembrokeshire coast.

He had confided in her simply because he had needed the use of her car, Angelica reminded herself as she walked back to the cottage. It would be stupid of her to look for a more personal reason, to allow her silly heart to imagine that he had told her because...

Because what? Because he loved her. Well, she knew already that that wasn't the case.

She stopped abruptly within sight of the cottages. Daniel... She ached for him so much, missed him so much, longed for him to return.

He had only been gone a couple of days. Today was the third day of his absence, and as yet it was barely lunchtime. The sun shone from a cloudless blue sky. She would make herself some sandwiches, take a book and go and lie on the beach, and if it was a poor substitute for being with Daniel, well, at least no one other than herself knew of it.

Half an hour later she was making her way down the narrow path that led from the cliff-top to the small secluded cove with its protective arms of sharp-toothed, jutting rocks which made it impossible for anyone to walk round from another beach to disturb her privacy.

Once she had eaten her lunch, the hot burn of the sun through the nylon of her swimsuit began to become uncomfortable, and, as she had done previously, she took it off, and then blissfully if somewhat

guiltily stretched out on the towel she had brought
with her, feeling the deliciously hot beat of the strong
sunlight warming her naked body.

The book she had brought with her couldn't hold
her interest; the combined effect of the heat and her
lunch was making her feel very sleepy. She rolled over
on to her stomach and closed her eyes.

It wouldn't do any harm just to catnap for a few
minutes. She was after all supposed to be relaxing,
resting, and if it helped to pass the time until Daniel's
return . . .

CHAPTER EIGHT

IT WAS the wave that woke Angelica, or rather the sensation of it breaking icily cold and wet against her spine, shocking her into an abrupt awareness that had her opening her eyes and rolling over in one swift, horrified motion as she realised how long she had been asleep and how dangerously fast the tide was coming in. She had been lying almost at the foot of the cliffs where their height gave the small cove the maximum amount of shelter, and even if she had noticed the tell-tale signs of the seaweed that clung to the cliffs some distance above her head, she doubted if she would have thought anything of it. It had not been her intention to fall asleep down here on the beach, nor to stay asleep for so long that the tide had turned and started to race in, covering the exposed sand, covering *her*, she recognised on a sudden jerky breath of panic as another, stronger wave came crashing down on top of her.

She scrambled to her feet, her hand going automatically to retrieve her basket and her swimsuit, but both of them had disappeared, swept away no doubt by the dangerous swirl of the tide. She was shivering now, chilled not just by the sea, but by fear as well. She wasn't in any real danger. She only had to climb the cliff path and within minutes she would be out of the tide's reach, but if she hadn't woken up when she did, if she had remained asleep for even another

fifteen minutes, her exit could have been blocked off
by the small channel of water she could already see
forming between her and the path. Now it was only
inches deep and she could wade through it with ease,
but had she left it any later...

Quickly wrapping herself in her now wet towel, and
securing it as best she could sarong-wise just above
her breasts, she headed for the cliff path, trying not
to think about what the sharp rocks could do to her
bare feet. She was lucky that all she was likely to suffer
was a few cuts and bruises. And, she added mentally
to herself as she slipped on the shale of the path and
had to pause to readjust her makeshift toga, that there
was no one about to witness either her folly, or her
undignified struggle to the top of the cliff.

She was within a few yards of reaching the cliff-
top when she suddenly discovered that she was not
after all alone.

After so many hours of longing for Daniel's return,
the sound of his voice from the cliff-top calling her
name ought to have filled her with delight, but instead it made her gasp with the horrified realisation
that far from returning to find her *soignée* and in
control of both herself and her life, he was about to
discover her half dressed, covered in damp sand with
her hair in tangles, her face free of make-up and her
knees and feet bearing the evidence of her scramble
up the hillside.

For a moment she toyed with the idea of pretending she hadn't heard him and staying where she
was virtually out of sight here under this small
overhang of cliff, but then he called her name again,

sharply and with such urgency that she automatically called back to him.

'What the——?' She saw him check as he came down the path towards her and saw her for the first time. The look on his face was one she found it impossible to interpret.

She could see anger—see it? She could practically feel the heat of it, and all that surprised her was that smoke wasn't coming out of his ears, but there was more there in his eyes than mere anger, and for a moment she remembered what he had told her about his father and felt a sharp spasm of guilt that he had had to come back after a visit to Cardiff which must have aroused all manner of unwelcome memories of his father's death, to find her in this semi-dangerous position.

'Daniel... I didn't expect you back this afternoon.'

She smiled cheerfully at him to reassure him, trying not to imagine the odd picture she must present huddled inside her wet towel, her hair all blown and tousled, her face hot from the sun and the climb.

Ignoring her casual greeting, he grabbed hold of her upper arms, making her wince as the strong pressure of his fingers rubbed the salt and wet sand into her sunburned skin.

As she winced and automatically tried to wriggle free of his hold, the loose knot she had tied in her towel gave way, and as Daniel released her and automatically stepped back from her in response to the demand contained in the movements of her body, she made a frantic grab for the towel, feeling the embarrassed colour scorch her skin as she failed and the rapid descent of her towel revealed to Daniel her sun-warmed body, its golden glow deepened and intensified by the hot burn of embarrassment that flooded swiftly down from her face, the whole length of her body, until she was actively curling her toes in an agony of mortification.

'What happened to your shoes?'

He was holding her towel and as she made to snatch it from him and wrap it quickly around her body, grimacing beneath its damp embrace, she told him crossly, 'They were swept away by the tide, like the rest of my things.'

'Like you could have been yourself as well. For God's sake, Angelica, have you no sense?'

'Of course I have,' she told him, stung by the accusatory condemnation in his voice. 'I was tired, I fell asleep, when I woke up——'

'Tired. Why?'

Cursing herself under her breath, she admitted reluctantly, 'I haven't been sleeping very well. I suppose I'm just not used to the silence here.'

She wasn't going to admit that her inability to sleep sprang from the fact that she had missed him so much that she hadn't been able to sleep and that today warmed by the heat of the sun, her exhausted body had finally given in to its need for the healing beneficence of the sleep it needed so much.

'You realise what would have happened if you hadn't woken up, don't you?' he demanded fiercely, adding as though she were a small child and incapable of comprehending, 'It wouldn't just have been your clothes and your shoes that were swept away. The tide in these small bays here is perilously strong.'

'But I did wake up,' Angelica told him firmly, spoiling the effect of her independence stance with a violent fit of shivering. They were standing out of the warmth of the sun, and, despite the brave face she was trying to assume for Daniel's benefit, it had been frightening to wake up and realise how easily her exit might have been cut off by the racing tide. She was not a very good swimmer; certainly nowhere near good enough to battle against a strong tide. And now she was both damp and cold, with reaction setting in to add to the chill already trembling through her body. The last thing she felt like right now was standing up for herself and being firmly independent. In fact what she really felt like doing, quite humiliatingly, was flinging herself into Daniel's arms and giving way to a hearty bout of tears, the kind she last remembered enjoying when she was six years old and had fallen off her new bicycle.

Almost as though this sudden mental memory of her childhood had somehow blocked her adult self-control, she felt the tears fill her eyes and roll unchecked down her face. One of them fell on to Daniel's hand, shifting his attention from her sore and scratched feet to her eyes. She saw his own widen, and then surprisingly witnessed the swift dilation of his pupils as though her emotionalism, far from irritating or embarrassing him, aroused a similar flood of emotion within him.

She shivered again, but this time not with cold, and then heard him curse as he stripped off the woollen shirt he was wearing and tugged impatiently at the knot on her towel, ripping its damp folds from her before she could stop him, and then bundling her into his shirt with a swiftness and ease that made her remember how often he must have performed this simple task for her in the days when she was so desperately ill with food poisoning. Certainly there was no awareness in his touch that her body was feminine and softly curved in all the places where his hands so objectively wrapped her in the blissful warmth of his shirt and then fastened it around her.

However, it was only when he picked her up in his arms that she finally thought to protest, saying huskily, 'No, Daniel. I can walk—your leg——'

'My leg is fine, which is far more than can be said for your feet,' he told her brutally, ignoring her added protests that she was far too heavy for him to carry and that she could manage on her own.

It was only when they had reached the top of the path and he had set her down on the grass that he derided, 'So you can manage on your own, can you? It certainly looks like it, doesn't it? I turn my back on you for two and a half days and you nearly manage to drown yourself, not to mention what you've done to your feet. You'll be lucky of you can walk on them by tomorrow morning, they're practically cut to ribbons. When we get back, you'll have to bathe them in salt and water. God knows what kind of infection you're likely to have picked up with open cuts like those.'

'Who knows, I might get to be really lucky,' Angelica muttered under her breath. 'I might get blood poisoning to go with my food poisoning.'

'Don't tempt fate,' Daniel advised her harshly. 'In your shoes . . .'

Angelica was tired of being lectured by him. If she was honest with herself all she really wanted was for him to pick her up in his arms again, for him to...

She sternly told herself that there was no point in letting her mind drift in that particular and very dangerous direction, that there was no point at all in letting her imagination furnish her with her far too vivid memories of what it felt like to be held and kissed by him.

Wriggling her bare toes in the grass, she reminded him wryly, 'I'm not wearing any shoes.'

It was warmer up here on the cliff-top, standing in the sun, sheltered from any breeze by the small copse of trees behind them. Daniel, who had been about to turn away from her, spun round so fast that it made her catch her breath.

'You little fool,' he said roughly. 'Do you *really* think it's a joke? You don't know these tides along here the way I do. You could easily have drowned.'

There was so much torment in his voice that instantly she felt ashamed and guilty. He was of course thinking still of his father, of the way he had died before he could help him, and her attempt to make light of her own plight must seem to him to be thoughtless and cold-hearted in the extreme.

She reached out and touched his arm placatingly, intending only to apologise to him, but the sensation of his sun-warmed bare skin beneath her questing fingertips made the muscles lock in her throat, such a wave of mingled love and longing sweeping over her that its pull was as strongly insidious as that of any ocean.

She started to apologise, her voice husky and low as she stumbled over the words, suddenly silenced as Daniel took hold of her and said rawly, 'Don't. It doesn't matter. You're safe, that's the important thing. When I couldn't find you at the cottage, I went to the farm. They said you'd mentioned that you'd been spending some time down here on the cove. As I came back I realised that the tide was on the turn—I stood up here and looked down into the cove, saw that the beach had been flooded by the sea. Have you any idea what that did to me? What you do to me?' he demanded savagely, and then before she could reply he was kissing her, not with tenderness or hesitancy, but with a mind-shredding intensity that left her with neither the ability nor the desire to do anything other than respond helplessly to the demand of his mouth.

And in truth wasn't this how she had dreamed of him kissing her, how she had ached for him to kiss her? she recognised as his hands slid into her hair, locking her beneath the fierce pressure of his mouth so that there was no way she could have avoided its intimacy even if she had wanted to do so. But she didn't want to do so. She wanted to stay right here where she was, her body against his, her mouth open to his, her hands smoothing eagerly over the powerful muscles of his back.

She could feel the warmth of the sun on her shoulder-blades, heating her skin through Daniel's shirt, but its heat was nothing compared to the heat within her.

'Angelica.'

She felt him whisper her name against her lips as they clung eagerly to his mouth. She bit dangerously

at his bottom lip as she felt his hands slacken their
grip, not wanting him to release her, not wanting to
let these precious moments of intimacy go. Ignoring
every anxious warning sent to her by her frantic brain,
she caressed his mouth with her own, her nails digging
urgently into the hard muscles of his back, deaf to
everything but the clamorous music of the desire that
beat through her.

Her long, lazy afternoon in the sun had relaxed her
inhibitions. Daniel's sudden and unexpected appearance had reactivated the desire she had thought
she had safely under control, and his anger, his
concern for her had been like a spark to dry tinder.

Scarcely aware of what she was doing, she clung to
him, raining tiny frantic kisses on his face until he
groaned and pulled her hard against his body, holding
her so tightly that she couldn't mistake the fierce throb
of arousal that pulsed between them.

'You want me.'

Her voice quivered slightly as she said it, triumph
mingling with an instinctive and primitive dart of apprehension. He would be her first lover... Her only
lover. Was she really ready for this? Was it really what
she wanted?

To make love here on the sun-warmed grass with
the cry of the sea birds in the distance and the soft,
lulling music of the ocean down below them; to
become one with Daniel here with all of the generous
bounty of nature all around them. To become his, not
in the shadowed darkness of a shuttered room, but
here in the warm, benign light of the sun. How could
she not want this? It was what she had been born for.

She bit gently on his earlobe, listening to the protest he groaned against her ear, smiling a secret woman's smile to herself when he told her thickly, 'This has to stop. And right now—if it doesn't . . .'

Delicately and yet with great precision she investigated the secret pleasures of his ear with the tip of her tongue, her own pulse accelerating as she felt the fierce, primeval race of his. He wanted her. Whatever else he might not feel for her, there was no mistaking this.

'Angelica.' He said her name slowly, harshly, as though each syllable was drawn out of him on a rack of tormented desire. 'We can't do this. We can't take the risk. I could make you pregnant.'

'No, it's all right. It's quite safe,' she lied to him, wondering, as she heard the words, what on earth had happened to her . . . Wasn't it supposed to be the man who urged the female to abandon caution and give in to passion—his passion? And yet here she was, blatantly lying to him, wanting him so much, loving him so much, that no price was too high to pay for the pleasure of having this special time of loving with him. And if she should conceive his child . . .

The fierce, elemental surge of wanting the thought brought shocked her even more than her earlier knowledge that she loved him. She wanted his child. Recklessly, foolishly, dangerously, against everything she believed in and had always lived by she wanted his child. Her child . . . her special gift from him. A child conceived out of this loving they would share. A child stolen from him, her conscience warned her, but she refused to listen to it, drowning it out with her own voice as she whispered heatedly in his ear,

'Make love to me, Daniel. Be my lover. Show me all the pleasures that I've never been able to know.'

She heard his indrawn breath, and thrillingly felt the surge of his body against her own, as it reacted immediately to her whispered pleas.

'I hope you know what you're doing,' he muttered thickly against her mouth as she turned to meet his kiss. 'Because there's no way I'm in any state to operate any kind of self-control. Have you any idea just what you're doing to me...or how much I want you?'

'No.' She feathered the word against his lips, taking little teasing bites at them, marvelling a little at her own daring, her own unexpected knowledge of how to be provocative and playful, of instincts she had never even guessed she possessed as she added softly, 'But I am hoping that you're going to show me.'

This time when he kissed her there was no holding back, no limiting of the need she could taste in the hungry possession of his mouth. When she felt his hands unfastening the buttons of the shirt he had so recently fastened around her, she knew immediately that this time there was no clinical restraint in their touch.

The wet sand had dried, rubbed off her skin by the warmth of his shirt, the sun had left her flesh blooming with soft colour. For the first time in her life a man was looking at her naked body with desire, and she knew immediately, without a word being said, that it *was* desire that darkened his eyes and made his hands tremble slightly as they skimmed her soft curves, lingering almost helplessly on the rounded globes of her breasts, tracing the aureole of her nipples subtly darkened by the sun.

'You've been sunbathing in the nude.'

His voice sounded unfamiliar, rusty and strained as though he was having difficulty in speaking.

'I couldn't resist it. The sun was so warm, and it was so private.'

'Just as I can't resist you,' he told her, the words muffled by the downward movement of his head as his mouth sought first one and then the other sun-darkened nipple.

Was it the effect of the sun that made them so sensitive? she wondered hazily, as liquid heat poured through her and her body arched convulsively beneath his protective hands while his mouth tugged feverishly on her pulsing flesh, so that with every frantic beat of her heart fresh spears of pleasure arced through her. When she closed her eyes against the brilliance of the sun, it only seemed to intensify the sensations rolling through her. Daniel's hands, Daniel's mouth, Daniel's body beneath her exploring fingertips, shuddering fiercely with each fresh caress she gave him.

She felt him lift her in his arms and place her tenderly on the warm grass, its scent rich and strong, mingling with the aromatic perfume of the wild thyme that grew along the cliff-top, but, sharpest and most erotic of all, the scent that was Daniel's alone, male, musky, aroused, and so pleasurable to her senses that she couldn't believe she had lived so many years without knowing its sensual familiarity.

She touched him wonderingly, amazed by how easily her slightest touch aroused him, lazily opening her eyes to watch him and to absorb the pleasure of looking at him while her fingertips stroked over him.

To her delight he made no attempt to conceal his reactions from her, letting her read in the rapid dilation of his pupils what his body was already telling her; that in this special moment of time he was as vulnerable and in need of her as she was of him. When he caught hold of her hand as she stroked her way down over the flat firmness of his belly, she tensed, watching him uncertainly as he carried her hand to his mouth and nibbled gently at her tightly curled fingers until the soft licking motion of his tongue made them relax and he was able to whisper against her palm, 'I want to make love to you more than I can remember wanting anything else in my whole life. I want to kiss you and taste you and show you all the pleasures that there are, but if you go on caressing me the way you are doing right now...' He hesitated, focusing on their joined hands, twining his fingers with her own as he added huskily, 'I want to take it slowly, gently... But it's been a long time. In fact——'

He stopped abruptly, even now hesitant about telling her that there had never been a woman like her, that while he had admired, respected and certainly liked the other women with whom he had made love, he had never felt about them the way he felt about her, he had never loved, ached for, hungered for them in the way he did for her. He had never loved them, and yet, even though she had been the one to instigate their lovemaking, even though everything about her told him that physically she was ready to be his lover, emotionally he was still unsure of her, unsure of why she wanted him. Unsure of how much commitment she was actually prepared to make to him.

What he *did* know was that he wanted a total commitment from her, that he wanted her in his life permanently, as his lover, his wife, the mother of his children, but something warned him against telling her this, against frightening her with the intensity of his feelings.

He didn't want to frighten her either emotionally or physically. He wanted to make this, her first time, so special for her that she would remember it all her life with pleasure and with joy, no matter what the eventual outcome of their relationship might be, and yet here he was with his body threatening to go totally out of control, threatening to behave like that of a callow boy. Now, when he needed all his experience, all his self-control, everything he had ever learned about her sex and how to pleasure it, he found his knowledge drowning beneath the rip-tide of need her lightest touch aroused in his own body. Even now, simply talking to her, he was conscious of how easily he could lose control . . . so totally, so completely that in her arms he would lose a little of himself.

Taking a deep breath, he told her unsteadily, 'In fact it might be a good idea if you—if you don't touch me. Not—not this time anyway.'

Not touch him. Angelica felt as though she had been slapped, as though she had done something wrong, something offensive, as though she had trespassed physically on to private territory. What was he trying to say to her? That he didn't *like* her touching him? That her touch repulsed him? Shades of the past, of Giles, of her own feelings of inadequacy flooded through her. She snatched her hand from his, turning her back on him, struggling to sit up until he took hold of her and shook her, saying huskily, 'Angelica, Angelica. It isn't that I don't *want* you to touch me, if that's what you're thinking.'

'Isn't it?' she demanded woodenly, refusing to look at him or to relax in his arms. 'You said——'

'I *said* it might be a good idea if you didn't, but not because I don't want you to.'

'Then why?' she demanded belligerently, refusing to accept the panacea he was offering her.

She heard him sigh and then say tautly, as he took hold of her hand and placed it against the most intimate part of his body, shocking her with both the simplicity and the immediacy of his actions, 'Because when you do, it makes me react like this, and so strongly that I doubt that I can control the effect you have on me long enough to get anywhere near making love to you, and certainly nowhere even close to the way I want to make love to you for your first time. I want to make it so slow and sweet for you, so special and memorable, I want to make it as perfect for you as I can, but every time you touch me my body goes so far out of control that I haven't a hope in hell of doing any such thing,' he concluded angrily.

Angelica could only stare at him, caught between shock and delight as she absorbed his words and recognised the truth and sincerity in them.

Without even thinking about what she was doing she held out her arms for him and begged tremulously, 'Daniel, please... I want you so much.'

She watched as his whole body tensed, dark colour burning up under his skin, a heat far more intense

than that held by the sun twisting through her as he
reached for her, smoothing the soft skin of her back
with hands that trembled as he muttered against her,
'Touch me now and I won't be able to hold you like
this.'

His mouth feathered along her throat, sending such
delicious ripples of pleasure welling through her that
she arched beneath his touch, as sinuously as a small
cat, soft sounds of delight tensing her throat muscles
as his hands stroked slowly and erotically over her
skin, skimming her breasts, caressing her waist and
then her hips, stroking the taut length of her thighs
and investigating the shadowed, sensitive hollows beneath her knees so that her breath jerked huskily in
her throat and her body flowered sweetly beneath his
touch, opening easily to his delicate, gentle intimacy.

When he stroked the soft, vulnerable flesh of her
inner thighs she gasped once and then quivered silently
in shocked pleasure at the realisation of how unbe-
lievably hungry she was for the gentle, rhythmic touch
of those sensitive fingers against the intimate heat of
her body, and how quickly she wanted more, far more
than that light caress.

Later she couldn't remember what she said or did
to communicate that need to Daniel, only that almost
by instinct he seemed to recognise it and answer it,
so that when she felt the first powerful thrust of his
body within her own she welcomed it with a soft, low
cry of pleasure, letting him guide her and harness her
feminine response to his need and her own so that the
powerful movement of his body became a rhythm
which seemed to echo the beat of her own blood, the
pound of her heart, even the sound of the ocean

breaking against the cliffs in a way that made her feel
so much at one with every force of nature within the
universe that it was as though she and Daniel between
them were that universe in miniature.

And then suddenly the pace of his lovemaking
changed, became more ardent, more urgent. She heard
him call out her name, saw the strong cording of the
muscles in his neck, felt the same fierce compulsion
grip her that was driving him and mindlessly, trust-
ingly, gave herself up to his domination, trusting him
so implicitly that the sensation of him driving deep
within her evoked only the most evocative and intense
emotions of closeness and unity, that the sudden ex-
plosion of sensation within her shattering that oneness
with him, splintering them into two separate voids
where the pleasure that pulsed so vibrantly through
her was something so immediate and so personal that
she could barely hear it echoed in the fierce sound of
exultation he made against her skin, just as her body
recognised and received the fierce pulse of his release.

She had a second's sharply intense awareness that
this brief span of time could change her life forever;
that in this brief second she could have received from
him the gift of a new life, a gift that her body would
cherish and harvest, and then stupidly she felt the
emptiness inside her where his flesh had been, a ter-
rible dolefulness swept over her, an emotional pain
and aloneness so intense that it made tears clog her
throat and sting her eyes.

Immediately Daniel was wrapping her in his arms,
muttering thickly, 'I'm sorry, I'm sorry, I didn't mean
to be so impatient, so—so rough . . . If I hurt you . . .'

If he *hurt* her... He would hurt her of course, but
not physically, not as he imagined. She tried to find
the words to tell him that, far from hurting her, he
had given her such pleasure, so much pleasure that it
was this that made her weep. Like a man glimpsing
the full radiance of the sun, only to know that he
would never see its like again and mourning that fact.
Just as she knew that never again in her whole life
would there be a time like this one. That there would
never again be a man like Daniel.

The knowledge made her tears flow more freely than
ever. She felt Daniel pushing her hair off her face,
stroking her damp skin, whispering soft words of
regret and concern into her ear, holding her against
the hard warmth of his body, the way she wanted to
be held for the rest of her life.

'Daniel,' she protested, suddenly conscious of their
nudity and the fact that they were after all in a public
place, but he seemed to misunderstand her concern
because, instead of releasing her, he simply held her
more tightly and told her huskily,

'Shush... It's all right, everything's going to be all
right. Next time...'

Next time... There was going to be a *next* time.
She went dizzy with the pleasure the thought conjured up.

'But first we've got to get you back to the cottage.
You can't walk back.'

She wanted to tell him that she could, that cut and
bruised feet were totally unimportant when you were
walking on air, but he was already wrapping her tenderly in his shirt, and then quickly dressing himself

before picking her up and, without listening to her protests, carrying her back towards the cottage.

There was so much she wanted to say to him, but she felt so dreadfully tired. She could actually feel her eyes closing no matter how hard she fought to keep them open. She yawned hugely, letting her eyes close...thoughts drifting in and out of her mind.

She and Daniel had made love. They were lovers. She might even have conceived his child, the child of the man she loved. It amazed her that she should feel so tranquil, so at peace with herself and the rest of the world...so completely at ease with the thought of having Daniel's child, even when she knew that she would be its sole parent. She would love it so much, just as much, if differently, as she loved Daniel himself.

Daniel. In so many ways it was as though she had known him all her life...been a part of him all her life. When she eventually left him it would be like losing a part of herself.

CHAPTER NINE

VERY carefully Daniel placed his precious burden down on her bed, and then slowly straightening gazed down into her sleeping face. No matter what the consequences of this afternoon, he couldn't regret the fact that they had made love. Tenderly he brushed the hair back off Angelica's face. When she had cried he had thought he had hurt her, until he had looked into her eyes and seen the dazed, incandescent pleasure that still glowed there. Then—then he had known, and his heart had turned over inside him with love and joy.

When he removed the hand that was cupping her face she moved restlessly in her sleep as though searching for him.

All the time in Cardiff he had been thinking about her, wanting to get back to her, and when he had eventually managed to wind up his final meeting ahead of schedule, instead of returning here in the morning as he had intended, he had decided to set out right there and then, driving as fast as safety allowed in order to get back to her.

To reach the cottage and find her missing had been like walking into a room and finding only cold, dead ashes in its hearth where one had expected the warmth of a fire. At first he had assumed she must have gone to the farm, but when he got there to be told that they hadn't seen her all day his feeling of disappointment and anxiety had sharpened into actual fear. A fear that for some reason she had left the cottage completely, perhaps gone back to London, to...

She said she no longer loved the other man and he believed that that was the truth; she could never have responded to *him* in the way that she had done if she truly loved someone else, but did she in her heart of hearts accept that she didn't love Giles any more?

He wasn't so sure. To hear from the Davieses that she might be on the beach had sent him hurrying back to find her.

The sight of that small cove under its surging cover of water as it was lashed by the incoming tide was something that would stay with his memory for the rest of his life, along with the anguish of believing that fate had repeated itself and that he was once again powerless to prevent the death of someone he loved. And then he had seen her struggling up the cliff path wrapped in that damp towel, her feet bare, her hair hanging down on to her shoulders, so that she'd looked more like a mermaid than a mortal woman, and all the emotions he had been holding under control since he'd first met her, since she had virtually collapsed into his arms on his doorstep, burst into frenzied life and he hadn't known which emotion was the strongest—his anger or his relief. All he *had* known was that he loved her so intensely that without her the rest of his life would be a meaningless emptiness, that his heart and soul would be laid to waste and would wither and die without her love to nourish them. And so he had ignored all the dictates of wisdom and caution and he had made love to her. Not as he had imagined doing in the privacy of a luxurious bedroom on a bed covered in clean, soft sheets, but on the sun-baked earth with the scents of nature all around them. And when he touched her it hadn't been with the finesse he had hoped for but with passion and need that had so overwhelmed him he had felt as though his inexperience were as great as her own.

Nothing in his life had ever come close to preparing him for the emotions he had felt when he held her in his arms, when he caressed her skin, when he felt her response to him as a man.

Tomorrow they would have to talk. The time for caution was gone, swept away by their tumultuous coming together. He looked down at the bed, tempted to lie down beside her, to wake up in the morning with her lying at his side, but there were still too many things they needed to sort out, and waking up in bed beside her was far more likely to lead to his making love to her again than it was to any kind of sensible, mature conversation.

He wanted so desperately to hear her saying that she loved him as much as he did her, but he wanted her to make that commitment freely, not to have it coerced from her.

Sighing faintly, he stood up. The specialist had been very hopeful about the way his torn muscles were starting to mend. With time and care, in another six months he would scarcely have any after-effects at all, and certainly no permanent damage, but he had warned Daniel against the effects of overwork, of stress and strain, pointing out that mental stress could have just as detrimental an effect on the human body as physical strain.

Daniel hadn't needed his warning. He had seen what the compulsion to devote too much time and energy to one's work had done to his father. For a long time he had battled against what he had known in his heart of hearts must be done ever since he had been approached by the large conglomerate who wanted to buy out the company. It had seemed so disloyal to his father to even contemplate selling out, and yet in this modern world it could be a very dangerous place for small businesses, especially ones as technically specialised as his father's.

In the end he had been forced to overcome his scruples, not for his own sake alone but also for the sake of his employees.

Their livelihoods would have so much more protection under the umbrella of their new parent company; he was to retain complete autonomy in the running of his father's company; he had been appointed chairman and managing director. He knew he had made the right decision, the only decision, and yet—and yet—he ached to be able to discuss his feelings, his guilt and anxiety over the fact that in many ways he felt he did not have the single-mindedness and purposefulness which had enabled his father to build the company out of nothing into the success it now was. He told himself that these were different times, that his skills were different from his father's; the guilt still remained. Angelica would understand them. He had picked up enough from their conversations to know that and he had wanted quite desperately to be able to unburden himself to her, to share with her the complexities of his feelings. He had envisaged returning to the cottage and initiating a gentle courtship, one that would not make her panic and flee from him, and yet what had he done virtually the moment he set eyes on her? He grimaced to himself as he turned to give one last reluctant glance towards the bed.

Tomorrow they would talk. Tomorrow...

Angelica woke up abruptly some time before dawn. Outside it was still dark, and a glance at her watch confirmed that it was barely three o'clock.

She moved uneasily beneath the duvet, conscious of sand particles irritating her skin and wondering what on earth they were doing in bed with her, and then abruptly remembering... everything.

She sat bolt upright in the bed, hugging her arms around her body until she realised that she was still wearing Daniel's shirt.

She tugged it off, shivering with a mixture of emotions, all of them so intense that cravenly she felt a desperate need to escape from them, to escape from herself, but most of all to escape from Daniel, and the questions he was bound to ask himself if not her in the cold light of day... questions he was perhaps already asking himself. Like why would a woman who by her own admission had never made love before, who had never particularly wanted to make love before, even with the man she professed to have fallen in love with, the man she was intending to marry, suddenly change so completely that, not only did she accept his lovemaking, but she had positively craved it, had wanted him with such an intensity that she had virtually begged him to make love to her, not cloaked by the softening privacy of the night's shadows, but in the full light of the sun, wanting him so intensely, loving him so intensely that she had never given a thought to the lack of protection their lovemaking involved, either outwardly or inwardly.

Her hands touched her stomach. She had told Daniel that she was sure she would not conceive, but she had lied to him. And in that her feelings had not changed. There was still a dangerously wanton ache inside her that told her how much she wanted to have conceived his child.

But she couldn't stay here in such close proximity to him. Not now.

It would be too dangerous, too potentially embarrassing for both of them. He was an intelligent man, a very intelligent man. It wouldn't be long before he guessed the truth. It wasn't so very hard to work out—after all, she must already have betrayed her love to him in a hundred or more small ways. Perhaps he had already realised how she felt about him, perhaps he had only made love to her out of pity and compassion knowing that he would never be able to return that love. Perhaps...

Her car stood outside in the moonlight. She had a spare set of keys. It would be easy enough to pack her few belongings and be gone long before Daniel woke up. Easy and surely the most sensible and sane thing to do... The best thing for *both* of them, she told herself firmly.

No matter how much she might love him, she had no intention of becoming a burden to him, of destroying what for her had been the most precious and wonderful moments of her life by seeing his kindness towards her change as he distanced himself from her. No, it was best to leave now while her memories were still intact, while she could still close her eyes and recall in perfect detail the look in his while he'd made love to her.

And besides, she dared not trust herself to stay without fearing that there would very soon come a time when it was no longer enough simply to be here with him, when she would want more... much, much more, when she would want to be held in his arms so desperately that she was ready to destroy her self-respect and everything that went with it. She couldn't endure the thought of seeing herself virtually begging for his touch, his love. Her mouth had gone dry, her heart was pounding with a frantic sick fear that told her how much she really wanted to stay here close to him, living on the hope that what had happened between them meant as much to him as it did to her, that he loved her in the same way that she loved him, but she knew it was impossible. If he had had any kind of feelings for her he would have told her so surely. It was the utmost folly to allow herself to dream hopeless dreams. No, better to go now, even if it did mean stealing away in the night like a thief.

Perhaps she *was* a thief—perhaps she had stolen from him the most precious gift a man could give a woman. His child. She shivered at the thought, desperately hoping it might be so, and almost equally desperately hoping it might not.

Financially she could support both herself and her child, but emotionally... Did she have that kind of strength, and what would happen when she had to leave her child in someone else's care while she returned to work? Would she have *that* kind of strength, the strength to leave Daniel's child with someone else, a someone else who might become more important in his or her life than she was herself? Did she have the right to allow herself to conceive, knowing that her child would never be able to claim its father...?

Hurriedly she stuffed her belongings into her cases, her fingers as urgent and frantic as her thoughts. She must not be here when Daniel woke up in the morning. She must not allow herself to weaken, to stay and perhaps break down in front of him and confess the truth.

What good would it do? He didn't love her, but he was a compassionate, caring man. Once she had admitted the truth, one of them would have to leave anyway, and it wasn't fair that it should be Daniel... No, it was better this way, and yet all the time she was carrying her bags downstairs, checking that she had left nothing behind, a part of her was desperately praying that Daniel would wake up, would see her and stop her.

It wasn't until she was finally sitting in the driver's seat of her car, the engine running quietly and smoothly, the cottages a dark blur against the lightening sky behind her, that she acknowledged that it was not going to happen, that even if he had heard her, Daniel was going to let her go, perhaps even wanted her to go.

When she finally emerged and reached the junction with the main road, she had to stop her car to wipe the tears from her eyes, her vision was so blurred.

Dawn was finally breaking. The worst dawn of her life, for all its translucent summer glory, with its promise of another hot, sunny day.

For her the dawn was grey with misery and pain, grey and shadowed like her thoughts, grey with that dull, miserable greyness of emptiness and defeat. The day stretched promisingly ahead, but not for her...for her the whole of her future was one bleak mass of grey emptiness, splintered here and there by those times of pain she would be unable to control, when she remembered a golden summer's afternoon, and the man who had shared it with her for the space of a handful of hours, who had taught her the true meaning of fulfilment, who had loved her physically with tenderness and passion, who had, please God, given her the precious gift of his child.

'But, darling, you said you were going to spend the whole of the summer in Wales... Your doctor——'

'I know, Mother, but I've changed my mind. If you can't put me up——'

'Angelica, of course I can, you know that. I'm only too pleased to have you here.'

She had come to Brighton on impulse, knowing instinctively that the less time she spent on her own, the better. They weren't expecting her back in her office for another month yet. Tom was away on holiday with his new love. There was nothing to draw her back to London, only the emptiness of her small house and the arid heat of a city summer.

At least here in Brighton she would have some company. She had been feeling guilty about how little time she had spent with her mother; here was her opportunity to rectify matters.

'You're still looking very peaky, darling. Are you eating properly? You're so thin...'

Repressing a sigh, Angelica assured her mother that she was fine, although in all honesty she had to admit that, of the two of them, despite the fact that she was twenty-five years her senior, her mother looked the happier and healthier.

In fact, she had seldom seen her parent looking so well, she recognised later on that day when they both sat down for lunch. There was a sparkle in her mother's eyes, a lilt to her voice, something in the way she laughed and moved that made her suddenly seem much younger than her fifty-odd years. She had even had her hair tinted, Angelica recognised, surveying the subtle highlights in her mother's hair.

'I'm afraid you'll find Brighton rather dull after London,' her mother told her as she urged Angelica to help herself to more food.

'You forget, I've been living in Pembroke for the last few days.'

'Yes, I know, darling. I must say I'm not totally surprised you've come back. We visited that coast once, your father and I, and it's very isolated. I have to admit that I was worried when you told me you were going to stay alone in some cottage miles away from anywhere. I mean, what if anything had happened to you—an accident?'

Angelica felt her body start to tremble. She put down her forkful of food untouched. 'I . . . I wasn't completely alone. There was someone, a man living in the cottage next door. Just as well, really,' she added, ducking her head over her plate, as she added as casually as she could, 'I was unfortunate enough to pick up some kind of salmonella bug on my way out there and came down with a pretty bad bout of food poisoning... He—Daniel—was marvellous, a true Good Samaritan.'

She was no longer even pretending to eat, giving in completely to her need just to talk about Daniel, as though in doing so somehow she was bringing him closer to her, as though somehow she was forging an invisible bond with him that nothing could ever break.

'Daniel—that's a good name,' her mother approved gently, watching her with eyes that saw more than Angelica realised. 'A strong-sounding name. Tell me about him.'

Angelica needed no further urging. The luxury, the need to do just that kept her speaking in brief, flurried, sometimes confusing sentences long after her mother had cleared her own plate, and explained a good deal that had puzzled Mrs Barnes when her daughter had first turned up on her doorstep so unexpectedly.

Angelica had always been such a private, contained child, never offering confidences, nor seeming to have any need to share her thoughts and feelings. Mrs Barnes had always thought of her as being closer to her father than to herself, and while she had regretted this she had accepted it. Now suddenly she was beginning to realise that she had perhaps been wrong... that it was insecurity and uncertainty that had made her daughter so reticent, and her heart ached compassionately for all that she sensed Angelica was not telling her.

She was in love with the man, of course, otherwise why this compulsive need to talk about him, why the incandescent look of pleasure-cum-pain that lit up her whole face every time she spoke his name? But what did *he* feel about Angelica? Her mother's instincts made her want to protect her child, to rescue her from potential pain, and yet she had to acknowledge that Angelica was an adult, and that it was not for her to interfere, nor to pass any comment on what she was being told. That all she could do was listen and only offer advice if it was requested.

Indeed she could sense as Angelica fell silent that already she was half regretting her confidences, half wondering if she had said too much, half wondering perhaps if she ought now to run away from her in the same way she had obviously run away from him, Mrs Barnes recognised wryly.

'Why don't I make us some coffee?' she suggested practically. 'And then afterwards, if you like, we could go and browse through a couple of antique shops. I need to find something for a friend's birthday. I know he's been looking for a fire screen for ages, and I thought I spotted just the thing the other day.'

In reality the last thing Angelica felt like was shopping, but she accepted her mother's suggestion, telling herself that the sooner she forced herself to accept that her time with Daniel was over and in the past, the better.

In the end Angelica spent more than three weeks with her mother, while she was there meeting not only her mother's friends, but also the man she suspected was going to become her stepfather. She liked him, and she liked the way he so obviously adored her mother, even if seeing them together was sometimes so unbearably painful that she ached to be completely alone.

She told herself that she had the rest of her life to live and that she could either wallow in self-pity or she could find a way of living that allowed her to accept that her life must go on without Daniel in it.

But it was a bitter blow to wake up one morning and discover that she was not after all going to have his child. Until that moment she hadn't realised how much she had been clinging to the frail hope that she would at least have his child to live her life for.

Now not only her present but her future as well had become aching voids of pain and loneliness. She had wanted so much to have conceived, and yet in reality wasn't it better that she had not done so?

No matter how logically she tried to reason she was still left with the feeling that fate had not considered her worthy of having Daniel's child, that it had found her wanting in performing this most basic and instinctive of all feminine functions, and that somehow in refusing to allow her to have Daniel's child fate had earmarked her as being flawed, not a complete woman. For the first time in her life she began to understand the torment suffered by women who for one reason or another could not conceive, something she had never imagined she would experience. Motherhood for her had always been something of an abstract state—fine for other people, but not something she had ever really wanted, and yet now suddenly, sharply, she did want it, ached for it, pined for it, loathed and resented the barren emptiness of the womb she had already mentally prepared for the nurturing of Daniel's baby.

Now even that dream, that hope had been snatched from her.

She had everything, and yet she had nothing, she thought emptily as she said her goodbyes to her mother and headed for London.

Tom would be back from France. Paul, her deputy, would be getting ready to hand back to her control of the company. It amazed her how little she was concerned with that. The business which had been the driving force in her life for so long now meant nothing to her. She was concerned for her employees, of course, concerned to maintain her father's good name and high standards, but for the first time she was forced to recognise that, given free will, running the company would never have been something she would have chosen to do. She had done it because she had felt it her duty, because she had felt if she did not do so she would be failing her father, and, while it was true that she would not envisage a way of life that would not in some way stretch and exercise her brain, she would have been quite happy to turn control of the company over to Paul on a full-time basis, taking only an advisory interest in it herself.

It was a sign of how little interest she had in what might be going on that, apart from a couple of duty telephone calls, she had made no attempt to check on what was happening in her absence, something unheard of at one time. She had driven herself so hard for so long that she had exhausted that part of her which had been responsible for creating that drive, she recognised tiredly, when she parked her car outside her small mews house and headed for the entrance.

Tom had laughed at her when she had first bought this house, but it had proved a wise investment, more than doubling in value. The trouble was though that it wasn't really a home, and she shivered as she unlocked her door and walked into the small hallway.

Even the air smelled over-clean and unused, arid and empty, tasting of sterility. She could never have brought up a child here. A child needed a garden, freedom, a home, not a collection of designer colour cued rooms, glossy enough to have featured in a high-profile modern magazine, and yet so empty of everything that made a home a home that Angelica almost felt as though she ought not to sit down on one of the pale cream coloured sofas.

Her apartment was cold and unwelcoming, she recognised critically, so pristine neat that it didn't look as though anyone could possibly live in it.

But then no one did. Not really. True, she slept here, but she rarely entertained friends here, preferring to dine out. She certainly never invited people round for lazy Sunday lunches... for casual get-togethers. The small garden had never even been used, and certainly not for the relaxed, easygoing kind of Sunday brunches the builders had undoubtedly envisaged.

Disliking her own thoughts, she reached for her answering machine and flicked it on.

As she had expected there were a dozen or so messages from those friends who did not realise she was away, plus a call from Tom letting her know he had returned, and asking her to get in touch with him. He was going to Yorkshire with his love for the weekend, he told her, adding that he would be back on Monday morning and that he wanted to speak to her urgently.

Monday morning. On Monday morning she was due to attend a conference, something she had been invited to months ago. She had no real desire to go, but she had made the commitment and she could hardly expect Paul to go in her place.

There was a final message from Paul confirming that he would call round in the evening as arranged to bring her up to date with everything that had been happening with the company during her absence.

The tape ran on into empty silence, and, although she played it back several times, nowhere on it was there the message she had been desperately hoping for, nowhere on it the sound of Daniel's voice. And yet why *should* he ring her? He was probably only too relieved that she had gone, thus saving them both the embarrassment of meeting again. And after all wasn't that why she had left in the first place? She had known really all along that he wouldn't get in touch with her of course. Of course she had. She had no idea why she had kept on playing that tape. It was obvious that he would not have tried to get in touch with her. Why should he?

Before leaving Brighton, her mother had taken her on a supermarket shopping trip, perhaps sensing that left to her own devices food was something she simply would not have bothered to buy. Had she been carrying Daniel's child, then she might have felt it necessary to ensure that she consumed a healthy diet, but now... It occurred to her that she was behaving as emotionally as a child refusing to eat in the hope that its behaviour would get it the attention it craved, and she told herself firmly that such behaviour was pointless and could only hurt herself.

Even so, she had no appetite for food, although she forced herself to prepare a simple supper dish shortly before Paul was due.

He arrived exactly on time, his warm smile changing to a slight frown as she let him in. 'You've lost weight,' he accused as he followed her into her small sitting-room. 'Are you sure you're not rushing back too soon? Stress can be a tricky thing.'

'Yes, especially when it's exacerbated by food poisoning,' Angelica agreed drily, explaining briefly to him what had happened, but this time omitting all mention of Daniel, just to prove to herself that she was capable of behaving like an adult.

After he had commiserated with her, Paul informed her that things had run reasonably smoothly in her absence. From the papers he laid in front of her, Angelica suspected that this was something of a tactful understatement, since it was obvious to her that he had run the company with skill and confidence, so much so that, had she discovered she was pregnant, she would have had little hesitation in appointing him to her own place as head of the firm and taking a less prominent role.

As she sipped her coffee, she wondered if perhaps she ought not to consider doing this anyway. He deserved both the promotion and the responsibility, and if *she* didn't offer it to him he might be tempted to go elsewhere. She made a mental note to discuss her thoughts with Tom, and when Paul asked her later if she was eager to get back into the driving seat, she made a small moue and said, consideringly, 'I'm not sure,' pleased to see the way his interest sharpened, although he was discreet in trying not to appear too curious. 'I've got this conference next week, of course.'

'Yes,' he agreed. 'I would offer to stand in for you since you don't seem to be fully recovered, but I'm off on holiday on Sunday, and I suspect Jean and the kids will disown me if I make any alteration to our arrangements.'

'And I wouldn't blame them,' Angelica told him firmly. Her own experiences over the last few weeks had shown her how important family ties could be, and how justified many wives were in complaining that their husbands devoted more time to their work than their homes and families. She was certainly not going to encourage any of her employees to become workaholics.

'Oh, by the way,' Paul told her when she was showing him the door, 'there've been a couple of personal calls for you. A man—he wouldn't leave his name, nor any message. He asked if we knew where he could get in touch with you. I knew you were at your mother's but it seems our mutual secretary for reasons of her own took it upon herself to refuse to give him that kind of information.'

Deanna had probably thought her caller was Giles, Angelica realised. Her secretary had been privy to certain details of her relationship with Giles—how could she not have been?—and Angelica suspected that her refusal to give away her mother's telephone number had sprung from a desire to protect her. But what if it had been Daniel trying to contact her? Her heart lurched, her pulse-rate rocketing.

'He—this man—didn't leave a name, then?' she enquired huskily.

Paul was frowning as he looked at her. 'Not as far as I know. Deanna only mentioned that he'd been on a couple of times because I happened to walk into her office while he was on the line...'

It couldn't have been Daniel; of course it couldn't. And even if it had, he had probably only been ringing out of good conscience, in the same spirit in which he had taken care of her, and in the same spirit in which he had probably made love to her, out of concern for a fellow human being, out of compassion for her as a woman, but not out of love, and certainly not out of the kind of all-consuming, all-encompassing love which was all that her aching heart would allow her to accept from him.

The way she felt about him, it had to be all or nothing. Anything in between would destroy her. Her own love was too intense, too strong to be satisfied with mere affection and friendship. It was a hungry, demanding love, a love that needed to be equalled if it was not to turn in upon itself and destroy her. No, it couldn't have been Daniel.

The weekend stretched emptily ahead of her. She had the conference to prepare for of course. It was a government-sponsored scheme for owners of those small businesses one of its departments had earmarked as being worthy of some special attention, companies which had in one way or another been successful enough in their particular fields to come under the department's avuncular eye.

Angelica had no desire to go, but she had accepted in the same spirit in which she had taken over the company in the first place—because she felt it was what her father would have expected of her.

One of the things she had discussed with her mother for the first time during her recent stay was her ambiguous feelings about remaining in control of the business. She had scrupulously pointed out to her mother that, if she took a less active role, it might mean a smaller income for them both, but her mother had astonished her by informing her that, following her father's death, she had been making a very nice living for herself dealing on the stock market, and that the income from the company had been safely banked with a large building society as a nest egg for Angelica herself.

'I've never felt happy about living off you, Angelica,' she had told her daughter. 'I didn't say anything to you because I didn't want to hurt your feelings. Your father always kept me wrapped in cotton wool.

'He was that kind of man and I never liked to tell him that I would have preferred a more robust partnership, that I would have liked to share his business life with him. He felt that wives had to be protected and supported, cosseted almost, but after his death ... well, I decided it was time I struck out on my own.' She had given Angelica a smile which was half mischievous and half rueful.

'I loved your father very much, but over the years he had devoted so much time to the company and so little to me. Well, I discovered that I rather liked my independence, so when you're making plans for your own future, Angelica, you don't have to consider me. I'm not decrepit yet, you know,' she had added in gentle reproof.

So if she did decide to step down from running the company, to take a more back-seat role, if it should mean a drop in their income, it wasn't going to bother her mother.

A few short weeks—that was all it had taken to show her what was really important in her life. And yet for all that she had genuinely believed herself in love with Giles, she had never for one second contemplated giving up running the company. She had never once then felt as she did now, that if Daniel had only loved her as she loved him she would gladly have given up everything to be at his side. Even if he had been, as she had thought, someone to whom the work ethic as she knew it simply did not exist.

But he didn't love her and he didn't want her. So why did she still feel this need, this urge to change her life so completely? Was it because she was afraid that if she didn't, eventually there might come a time when her work was *all* that her life held? She gave a tiny shiver, not liking the pictures her mind was drawing for her.

Once this conference was behind her then she would sit down with Tom and discuss what was in her mind, she promised herself.

CHAPTER TEN

THE weekend dragged by. Angelica had lost all hope of Daniel's contacting her now, and in some contrary way was almost glad that he hadn't done so, because if he had... If he had, the temptation to see him would have been so great, so overwhelming that she doubted that she would have been able to stop herself from driving down to Pembroke to be with him, and once she was with him how long would it have been before she had been pouring out her heart to him, pleading with him for whatever scraps of affection and compassion he could give her?

And that wouldn't be fair to either of them. If she tried to bind him to her with chains of guilt and compassion, she would never be able to live with herself and ultimately there would come a day when he would resent those chains she had forged, when he would resent her.

No, it was better this way. Far, far better. Let him think her ungrateful, unbalanced even, but please God never let him think her pathetic or pitiable.

The conference was being held in a smart country house hotel close to Bath. Angelica set off in good time for the pre-lunch introductory talk, and found when she eventually got there that she was one of the first to arrive.

A smiling receptionist handed her an elegant folder containing all the details of the conference, and gave her the key to her room.

The government department concerned had taken over the entire hotel for the three days of the course, but Angelica was dismayed to see that some substantial blocks of free time were written into the timetable. The hotel was set amid beautifully landscaped grounds; if she had not been here on her own...if Daniel had been with her for instance, if they had been here on holiday, this place would have been idyllic. As it was...

She was just about to take her case up to her room when the receptionist suddenly called her back. She was frowning, as she listened to something a dark-suited young man was telling her. He was, Angelica noticed, wearing a badge bearing the words 'Assistant Manager'.

'I'm sorry,' the receptionist apologised to her. 'There seems to have been a slight mix-up with the rooms and I've given you the wrong key.'

As Angelica handed hers back to her, she handed her another, apologising again. Angelica gave her a wan smile. It really didn't matter to her what her room was like. Nothing mattered to her any more.

Even so, it startled her to discover she had been given, not merely a room, but a private suite with its own sitting-room, comfortably furnished with deep, squashy sofas, covered in soft chintz to match the curtains at the windows, windows that gave her a wonderful view of the park and its man-made lake. In the middle of the lake was a small island, complete with a temple.

Turning away from the window, Angelica walked into her bedroom. It was larger than she had expected, and beautifully furnished with excellent and no doubt expensive reproduction Georgian furniture, including a very handsome four-poster bed, lavishly draped with the same chintz as her sitting-room.

Beyond the bedroom was an equally well-appointed bathroom, with a huge old-fashioned bath. The walls were painted with a mural, depicting various vaguely Italianate scenes, the whole ambience of the suite so luxurious and expensive that Angelica could only marvel that *she* had been given it. She dreaded to think how much it must normally cost to spend even one night in such opulent surroundings.

She had heard that the chef-owner of the hotel had an excellent reputation and that the small weekend dinner dances held here were always booked up months in advance.

She had travelled to Bath in a smart, businesslike suit, and apart from checking that her hair and make-up were discreetly in order there was no reason for her to delay going downstairs to join the others.

The same receptionist who had given her the key directed her towards the conference-room.

There was no one there whom she recognised, although some of the men, those who obviously knew one another, were gathering together in small groups, while another group, this time comprised of members of her own sex, was also steadily gathering in one corner of the room.

Wondering if she ought to go and join them, and wishing she could summon a little more enthusiasm for something she knew quite well would once have demanded her fullest concentration, she hesitated, looking uninterestedly around the room, refusing the coffee she was offered. And then another small group walked into the room, obviously the government officials, and the conference began in earnest.

There was a brief break for lunch, and then a talk in the afternoon about the various methods of succeeding in selling in Japan, complete with helpful advice about the best way to find a Japanese interpreter.

Angelica listened vaguely, knowing guiltily that her place on the conference could and should perhaps have gone to someone else who would make better use of it.

After afternoon tea there was a discussion group to which she contributed almost next to nothing, and then a break before a formal dinner being given during the evening at which their guests would be some visiting Japanese businessmen.

Angelica changed for dinner without enthusiasm. The slim-fitting plain black dress she had brought with her hung loosely on her body, making her sharply aware of how much weight she had lost, and was still losing. As she studied herself in the mirror she acknowledged that she looked tired, drained, lifeless almost. If Daniel could see her now he would be only too relieved not to be involved with her. She made a mental note to avoid wearing black in future. It seemed to underline her unhappiness. She looked like a widow wearing mourning weeds.

Formal banqueting tables had been arranged in the dining-room. Angelica was not surprised to discover she was seated halfway down one of these well away from the top table. The men to either side of her were strangers to her as were those opposite her, although the seat immediately opposite hers was empty. Someone who was obviously running a little late.

The top table filed in, the Japanese businessmen were introduced and discreetly applauded. Everyone sat down, and Angelica tried to make sensible responses to the questions being posed by her dinner companions.

She toyed with her soup, barely drinking any of it much to the obvious disgust of the rather portly man to her right, and then, just as the staff were clearing the tables for the next course, there was a small flurry of activity and someone sat down in the seat opposite her...

No, not someone, she recognised as her heart gave a frantic bound and her whole world seemed to turn upside-down... Not *someone* at all—but Daniel.

A Daniel she scarcely recognised in his dark grey business suit and crisp white shirt, his dark curly hair tamed and groomed, his wrists and hands darkly tanned, hard and very male in comparison to the over-plump, flaccid flesh of the men seated either side of her.

Her heart was pumping far too fast. He hadn't seen her yet. He was saying something to the woman on his left, smiling at her as he shook his head, no doubt explaining why he was so late in arriving.

Above the general level of conversation Angelica caught the words, 'last-minute arrangement... got delayed'.

Any minute now he was going to turn round and see her, and when he did...

On the pretext of losing her napkin, she ducked her head and tried frantically to decide what she should do. The last thing she felt capable of doing right now was confronting him across a table, and pretending...pretending what? That she didn't know him? Of course she couldn't do that. What, then? Smile and say cheerily, 'Heavens, what a coincidence.' As though they had parted on the best of terms, as though that fierce, elemental coming together had never taken place, as though they were nothing more than the merest chance met acquaintances. Well, if not that what were they? Lovers?

Hardly. Friends? No, not really.

'I say, are you all right? Looking a trifle peaky—wondered if you felt quite the thing?'

The words were like manna from heaven. Instantly she chided herself for not being nicer to her plump neighbour earlier. Now he had given her the perfect excuse to escape. Shaking her head, she pressed her napkin to her mouth and watched as he went slightly pale.

He was no Daniel. Doubtless the thought of her being publicly unwell would embarrass the life out of him.

'So sorry,' she managed to say. 'I think——'

'Yes. Shouldn't stay here if I were you. Go up to your room. Soon feel more the thing.'

Without daring to turn to see if Daniel had recognised her, she fled, as discreetly as she could, pausing only in Reception to explain to the girl on duty, a different girl this time, that she had only recently recovered from a bout of food poisoning and that she was not feeling too well.

'If you should want a doctor,' the girl offered, but Angelica shook her head.

'No, really I'll be fine. I think it was just the smell of the food,' she lied guiltily.

Upstairs in her suite she locked the door and then stood shivering in the middle of the room. Daniel here. That was the last thing she had expected, and no doubt he would have been equally shocked to see her. More shocked, no doubt. Even now, knowing that the most sensible thing she could do was pack her bags and leave right now, all she really wanted to do was to find out which was his room, to see him, to talk to him, to be with him. But she *couldn't* give in to that kind of temptation. And neither could she leave the course, not without some kind of explanation. But she already had her explanation—her food poisoning. If she left now before the dinner was over...

In her absence someone had unpacked her things. She raced round the bedroom feverishly flinging them back into her suitcase, not hearing the soft turn of a key in the outer door, not realising she wasn't alone any longer, until some sixth sense made her look up.

'Daniel.' Her hand went to her chest and her heart started to pound. 'What...? How did you...?'

She stared at him in disbelief, dropping the skirt she was holding. He was standing in the doorway to her bedroom, looking both agonisingly familiar and yet in so many ways unfamiliar and unknown, in the dark formality of the business suit in which he looked as completely at home as he had done in his worn jeans.

Something about him was different though. His face was thinner, older somehow, his eyes darker, shadowed, as though he had endured recent suffering.

'I should have guessed you'd do this, shouldn't I?' he demanded, ignoring her questions. 'You seem to make a habit of running away. Hardly flattering... What is it you're running from, Angelica? Me or yourself?'

She couldn't stop staring at him, greedily drinking in each tiny detail, aching to be able to go up to him and touch him, just to reassure herself that he actually was real. His angry words barely impinged on her awareness. Daniel here. Daniel actually here.

'Where exactly are you going?'

Where was she going? She frowned as she looked away from him. His unexpected presence in her suite had momentarily thrown her off guard. She couldn't allow him to guess the truth.

'I'm not feeling very well,' she lied. 'I—I've—decided to go home. The conference wasn't a good idea anyway. I should have cancelled and let Paul come instead. Once he takes over from me——'

'You're letting someone *else* take over the company.' Daniel was frowning now.

'Yes. Yes.'

'Why?' He shot the question at her, and then abruptly his face changed, becoming so hard and menacing that she actually felt a tiny thrill of fear.

'You lied to me, didn't you? You're pregnant, aren't you? You're having my child. Well, that does it. You're marrying me, Angelica, whether you like it or not. A child needs a father, and if it means keeping you chained to my side from now until I can get a special licence, *you* are going to marry me. My child isn't going to grow up without knowing me. I don't care how modern that might be.'

Angelica sank down on to the bed, too shocked to conceal her feelings.

'What is it? What's wrong?' Daniel demanded urgently, when he saw the tears spring to her eyes.

She shook her head, too overcome to respond, and then gasped as she felt his hands on her shoulders, shaking her gently, tenderly almost.

'My love, I'm sorry if I frightened you, but you must see it for yourself... You *can't* deprive our child of its right to know both its parents.'

She swallowed painfully, and told him huskily, 'Daniel, there isn't going to be any child.'

He released her immediately, the look on his face so bitter, so filled with pain that she almost reached out and touched him, but then she was glad she had not done so when he accused, 'You did that. You destroyed our child.'

For a moment she couldn't believe what she'd heard. She stood up and pushed past him, her own anger matching his as she told him fiercely, 'You're wrong, Daniel. More wrong than you can possibly believe. If I *had* conceived your child...' She swallowed back the words which would have told him how much that child would have meant to her and how much *he* meant to her and said unsteadily instead, 'What I was trying to tell you was that there never *has* been any child.'

'Then why are you giving up the company? Why did you run away from me just now?'

She wanted to lie to him, to make some easy excuse, but the words locked in her throat. She had suffered too many shocks to be able to think straight, never mind manufacture convincing lies.

'I thought it was best,' she managed eventually. 'I thought it was best for both of us. That you wouldn't want to see me.'

'That *I* wouldn't want to see you? My God, woman ... You run away from me in the middle of the night, after the most perfect loving I've ever known. You disappear completely without trace. Your secretary refuses to tell me where you are. Tom can't be contacted because he's out of the country—or at least he was. Thank God he returned in time to tell me you'd be coming here, or doubtless I'd still be trying to track you down. I'd even got to the stage of actually thinking I was going to have to storm that damned office of yours.

'I repeat, you run away from me, and you keep *on* running and you have the gall to accuse me of not wanting to see you. Be honest with me, Angelica,' he demanded roughly, 'I've *got* to know. Did that afternoon—do *I* mean anything to you, anything at all?'

Without waiting for her response, he turned round so that she could only see his back, his bunched shoulders set with defeat and something else that made her heart twist painfully inside her.

'I told myself I wouldn't push you. That you needed time to get over Giles properly, that I wouldn't panic you into rejecting me before you'd had a chance to get to know me, to, or so I hoped, come to feel just a tenth of what *I* feel for you in return, and then I

went and blew it all, didn't I? Then I went and messed
the whole thing up by letting you know well and truly
how much I cared, how desperately I love you——'

Angelica couldn't believe what she was hearing.
'You love me?' she interrupted him shakily.

He turned round and looked at her, saying self-
mockingly, 'No, of course I don't. I always make love
the way I made love to you... I always lose control
like that, I always need to be with someone so much
that I cancel meetings and alter schedules, just so that
I can rush back to her, I always pester secretaries, and
ring up strangers demanding addresses, I always get
myself on to conferences I've no business attending.
Of course I love you, you fool. But I'm the one who's
the fool, aren't I? I can't go on like this. I have to
know. Is there any possibility that you could come to
love me? I know you want me.' He saw her face and
smiled gently at her. 'No, don't deny it. And don't
feel ashamed of it either. There's nothing to be
ashamed of in natural, healthy desire, but I want more
than your desire, my angel... I want your love—all
of it.'

'You've got it,' Angelica told him huskily, and felt
the tears burn her eyes as she saw the way her words
transformed him.

'You mean that—you really mean it?' he demanded thickly, taking hold of her. 'Oh, my God, if
you're lying to me...'

'I'm not—that's why I left, because I knew I loved
you, and I was terrified of betraying it to you. I was
so convinced that you couldn't love me, that you only
felt compassion for me, pity.'

'After the way we'd just made love?' he demanded
wryly.

She flushed a little and reminded him, 'I'd nothing
to compare your lovemaking with. I thought . . . Well,
you said it had been a long time.' She discovered that
she was blushing and laughing a little herself when he
touched her hot face with one forefinger, caressing
her overheated skin.

'Abstinence had nothing to do with the way I reacted to you, nothing at all.'

His mouth was unbearably close to her lips. She
only needed to move a fraction of an inch, less than
that, to feel its familiar heat. She stroked its male
outline with the tip of her tongue and whispered lov-
ingly to him, 'I wanted to conceive your child. I told
myself that if I couldn't have you, then at least having
your child would mean I had a part of you . . . How
could you think I could ever have destroyed that kind
of gift?'

'How could you ever think *I* didn't love you? We've
both been fools. If we'd been honest with one another
from the start . . . If I'd told you how I felt about you,
but I thought it was too soon. When you told me
about Giles, you were so determined not to allow
yourself to love another man, I thought it was going
to take me months to break down the barriers you'd
built up around yourself.'

'When in reality they'd already crumbled and I was
hopelessly in love with you.'

'You concealed it very well.'

He kissed her slowly and deeply, making her tremble
with need and move closer to his body, seeking the

familiar heat of its arousal, and sighing softly under his kiss when she found it.

'I can't believe you deliberately invited yourself on to this conference just to see me,' she told him huskily minutes later.

'Well, you'd better.'

He was kissing her again.

'I'm surprised they had a spare place, and a spare room—it was pretty heavily booked.'

'Mmm. They didn't—have a spare room, that is—but when I explained to them I'd be sharing your room and booked us both this suite . . .'

'*You* booked this suite?' She broke free of his kiss and stared at him in disbelief.

'Mmm.'

He leaned forward and started to nibble the sensitive cord in her neck, sending her thoughts into chaotic disorder.

'You were so sure of me, then,' she protested.

'No, just so desperate that I was determined that somehow or other I'd manage to get you on your own, somewhere where you couldn't run away from me. If necessary I'd have spent the night on th. sofa. If necessary I still will,' he added gravely, cupping her face with his hands and looking down into her eyes. 'I want you forever, Angelica, not just for the space of a few brief nights.'

She was trembling beneath his hands, knowing that he was speaking the truth. 'It seems a shame to waste such a wonderful bed,' she told him shyly . . .

'Yes, it does, doesn't it? Do you know that when I initially envisaged making love to you I wanted it to be in a room like this . . . rich and luxurious, with the kind of bed that's just made for lovers. I wanted to take my time with you, to make love to you slowly and lingeringly so that for the rest of our lives you'd know how much you mean to me. Instead . . .'

'Instead, nothing,' Angelica told him fiercely. 'What happened between us was wonderful, open and natural, instinctive and somehow totally right . . . Even when I thought that you didn't love me, I knew that physically you had loved me, that what we'd shared had been special, if only in the physical sense, and I certainly don't regret a second of it. Well, at least not now. I did regret the fact that, even though I'd lied to you, I hadn't conceived.'

'Mmm. I think after tonight we'd better get married just as soon as it can be arranged. We can make pressure of mutual business commitments our excuse,' he told her quietly, frowning. 'You mustn't think that I'm going to expect or want you to give up running your father's company, unless you want to. I've sold out my controlling interest in my business. I'm still based in Cardiff, but I'm quite prepared to tell my parent company that I've changed my mind about staying on as MD, and looking for a job in London instead . . .'

Angelica shook her head. 'No. I've come to realise that the company was only important to me as a duty, a responsibility. I want time to spend with you, with our children. I'd already decided to ask Paul if he'd like to take over for me. What I'd really like is a house in the country, somewhere with a bit of land, perhaps even close to the sea.'

'Mmm. What I'd like right now is to take you to bed and make love to you, just to make sure you're actually real, that this isn't just something I'm imagining.'

It was a long, long time later when Angelica suddenly remembered the conference. Snuggled in Daniel's arms, she asked him sleepily, 'Do you think they'll have missed us?'

'Not anything like as much as *I've* missed you these last weeks. If you ever run away from me again...'

'I won't,' she assured him softly, and then kissed him gently.

He kissed her back, not gently at all, and as she felt her body quicken with renewed pleasure she gave mental thanks to the wondrous powers of fate for bringing them so miraculously together, for knowing how perfect they were going to be for one another.

HARLEQUIN PRESENTS®

IF YOU THOUGHT ROMANCE NOVELS WERE ALL THE SAME...LOOK AGAIN!

Our new look begins this September

It's difficult to improve upon the best, but we have! This September, Harlequin will introduce a new and brighter cover to enhance the look of Harlequin Presents.... Consistently intense, passionate love stories that take you around the world ... written by our leading international romance authors.

Watch for a sneak preview of our new covers next month!

HARLEQUIN PRESENTS—
The world's bestselling romance series!

Back by Popular Demand

Janet Dailey

Americana

Janet Dailey takes you on a romantic tour of
America through fifty favorite Harlequin
Presents novels, each one set in a different
state, and researched by Janet and her husband,
Bill.

A journey of a lifetime. The perfect collectable
series!

August titles   **#37 OREGON**
To Tell the Truth

#38 PENNSYLVANIA
The Thawing of Mara

OFFICIAL RULES • MILLION DOLLAR MATCH 3 SWEEPSTAKES
NO PURCHASE OR OBLIGATION NECESSARY TO ENTER

To enter, follow the directions published. If the "Match 3" Game Card is missing, hand print your name and address on a 3"×5" card and mail to either: Harlequin "Match 3," 3010 Walden Ave., P.O. Box 1867, Buffalo, NY 14269-1867 or Harlequin "Match 3," P.O. Box 609, Fort Erie, Ontario L2A 5X3, and we will assign your Sweepstakes numbers. (Limit: one entry per envelope.) For eligibility, entries must be received no later than March 31, 1994 and be sent via first-class mail. No liability is assumed for printing errors, lost, late or misdirected entries.

Upon receipt of entry, Sweepstakes numbers will be assigned. To determine winners, Sweepstakes numbers will be compared against a list of randomly preselected prizewinning numbers. In the event all prizes are not claimed via the return of prizewinning numbers, random drawings will be held from among all other entries received to award unclaimed prizes.

Prizewinners will be determined no later than May 30, 1994. Selection of winning numbers and random drawings are under the supervision of D.L. Blair, Inc., an independent judging organization, whose decisions are final. One prize to a family or organization. No substitution will be made for any prize, except as offered. Taxes and duties on all prizes are the sole responsibility of winners. Winners will be notified by mail. Chances of winning are determined by the number of entries distributed and received.

Sweepstakes open to persons 18 years of age or older, except employees and immediate family members of Torstar Corporation, D.L. Blair, Inc., their affiliates, subsidiaries and all other agencies, entities and persons connected with the use, marketing or conduct of this Sweepstakes. All applicable laws and regulations apply. Sweepstakes offer void wherever prohibited by law. Any litigation within the province of Quebec respecting the conduct and awarding of a prize in this Sweepstakes must be submitted to the Régies des Loteries et Courses du Quebec. In order to win a prize, residents of Canada will be required to correctly answer a time-limited arithmetical skill-testing question. Values of all prizes are in U.S. currency.

Winners of major prizes will be obligated to sign and return an affidavit of eligibility and release of liability within 30 days of notification. In the event of non-compliance within this time period, prize may be awarded to an alternate winner. Any prize or prize notification returned as undeliverable will result in the awarding of that prize to an alternate winner. By acceptance of their prize, winners consent to use of their names, photographs or other likenesses for purposes of advertising, trade and promotion on behalf of Torstar Corporation without further compensation, unless prohibited by law.

This Sweepstakes is presented by Torstar Corporation, its subsidiaries and affiliates in conjunction with book, merchandise and/or product offerings. Prizes are as follows: Grand Prize—$1,000,000 (payable at $33,333.33 a year for 30 years). First through Sixth Prizes may be presented in different creative executions, each with the following appproximate values: First Prize—$35,000; Second Prize—$10,000; 2 Third Prizes—$5,000 each; 5 Fourth Prizes—$1,000 each; 10 Fifth Prizes—$250 each; 1,000 Sixth Prizes—$100 each. Prizewinners will have the opportunity of selecting any prize offered for that level. A travel-prize option, if offered and selected by winner, must be completed within 12 months of selection and is subject to hotel and flight accommodations availability. Torstar Corporation may present this Sweepstakes utilizing names other than Million Dollar Sweepstakes. For a current list of all prize options offered within prize levels and all names the Sweepstakes may utilize, send a self-addressed, stamped envelope (WA residents need not affix return postage) to: Million Dollar Sweepstakes Prize Options/Names, P.O. Box 4710, Blair, NE 68009.

For a list of prizewinners (available after July 31, 1994) send a separate, stamped, self-addressed envelope to: Million Dollar Sweepstakes Winners, P.O. Box 4728, Blair, NE 68009.   MSW7-92